Mayor
of the
Roses

STORIES

The Miami University Press
Poetry Series

General Editor: James Reiss

The Bridge of Sighs, Steve Orlen
People Live, They Have Lives, Hugh Seidman
This Perfect Life, Kate Knapp Johnson
The Dirt, Nance Van Winckel
Moon Go Away, I Don't Love You No More, Jim Simmerman
Selected Poems: 1965-1995, Hugh Seidman
Neither World, Ralph Angel
Now, Judith Baumel
Long Distance, Aleda Shirley
What Wind Will Do, Debra Bruce
Kisses, Steve Orlen
Brilliant Windows, Larry Kramer
After a Spell, Nance Van Winckel
Kingdom Come, Jim Simmerman
Dark Summer, Molly Bendall
The Disappearing Town, John Drury
Wind Somewhere, and Shade, Kate Knapp Johnson
The Printer's Error, Aaron Fogel
Gender Studies, Jeffrey Skinner
Ariadne's Island, Molly Bendall
Burning the Aspern Papers, John Drury
Beside Ourselves, Nance Van Winckel

Introducing
The Miami University Press
Fiction Series

Edited by The Creative Writing Faculty of Miami University

Mayor of the Roses, Marianne Villanueva
Project Editor: Brian Ascalon Roley

MAYOR OF THE ROSES

STORIES

Marianne Villanueva

Miami University Press
Oxford, Ohio

Library of Congress Cataloging-in-Publication Data

Villanueva, Marianne, 1958-
  Mayor of the Roses : stories / Marianne Villanueva.
    p. cm. -- (Miami University Press fiction series)
    ISBN 1-881163-45-8 (cloth, alk. paper) – ISBN 1-881163-46-6 (pbk, alk. paper)
    1. Philippines--Social life and customs--Fiction. 2. Filipino Americans--Fiction. I. Title.
II. Series.

PR9550.9.V49M39 2004
823'.914--dc22   2004057124

The paper in this book meets the guidelines
for permanence and durability of the Committee
on Production Guidelines for Book Longevity
of the Council on Library Resources ∞

Printed in the U.S.A

9 8 7 6 5 4 3 2 1

ACKNOWLEDGMENTS

The following stories have been previously published, some of them in a slightly different form: "Mayor of the Roses" in *Virtual Lotus: A Southeast Asian Anthology* (2002); "Sutil" in *The Threepenny Review* (Fall 1995); "Extinction" in *ZYZZYVA* (Spring 2001); "Mountains" in *The Literary Review* (Spring 2000); "Lenox Hill, December 1991" in *Charlie Chan is Dead: New Asian American Writing* (1993); "Infected" in *Tilting the Continent: Southeast Asian American Literature* (2000); "Black Dog" in *Fourteen Hills* (Summer/Fall 1997); "Wanting" in *Puerto del Sol* (Spring 2001); "Bad Thing" in *Into the Fire: Asian American Prose* (1996); "Silence" in *The Threepenny Review* (Winter 1997).

TABLE OF CONTENTS

MAYOR OF THE ROSES

I grew up in a country of torrid heat, a country that, if I were to try and describe it, might be summed up simply by saying that the smells were not like anything we know here. The smells I remember were pungent smells of raw meat, blood, and rotting garbage, of human sweat. The sun beat down constantly.

In that country, I heard stories. It didn't matter whether they were true or untrue. The last time I was home, visiting Manila, I asked my mother, "What ever became of your friend, the one who had all her clothes stolen during a hold-up?"

My mother froze. She looked at me. "What are you talking about?" she said. "I never had a friend who had her clothes stolen."

"Yes," I told her. "You said she was picked up outside a bank, while she was using the ATM machine. A car of men. They dropped her off on Makati Avenue, without her clothes."

No, my mother said. No such thing ever happened.

So where did this story come from? I couldn't have pulled it out of my head. I always had this picture of a middle-aged woman, breasts dangling, being kicked out of a car, right in the heart of the commercial district. At least, I used to think, the men didn't do anything to her. They wanted to humiliate her, but she wasn't raped.

———————

In the province of Laguna is a small town called Calauan. It is near the University of the Philippines at Los Baños, where my family used to go to buy the famous Laguna cheese, and milk that tasted as close to American milk as my mother could find in the Philippines. In this place, a decade ago, seven men gang-raped a young beauty queen from the University of Los Baños.

1

My mother said, "They used her vagina as an ashtray. Did you know that?"

My grandmother said, "Afterwards, there were seven different kinds of semen in her body."

My mother added, "I heard there was a whole pillowcase stuffed down her throat."

We were having dinner, I recall, at the time of this conversation. The maids were passing around dishes. Perhaps one of my younger brothers was present.

———————

I never knew anyone who came from that place. We'd stop sometimes at a gas station to ask for directions. Sometimes we bought pots for plants from shacks set up by the side of the dusty roads. The people were dark and thin; they were like the people of any small town we passed through on our way to the mountains or the beach. I never even knew anyone who went to the University there. So when I first read about the case in the papers, I couldn't quite imagine the victim's face. What I saw in my mind was this: long dark hair; oddly, a tiara; a ball gown. Later, when I saw a picture of her in the newspapers, she didn't look at all the way I had expected. That is, she wasn't extraordinarily pretty.

The men were different. The men I could imagine. They had secretive eyes, always. They threw dice and drank beer and had bellies that hung over the cinched belts of their tight khaki pants. They had loud, slurred voices.

The Mayor himself, the chief perpetrator, was a caricature. When I saw him for the first time, in the courtroom, I thought he was wearing a rug on his head.

That first day, the courtroom was close and noisy. Cigarette smoke hung in the air, obscuring the face of the woman who presided in her judge's robes. The light slanting in from the louvered window shades was filled with dust motes.

I was dazzled by the play of light and dark on the people's

faces. I knew no one there. I had come merely as an observer. Because of the stories.

The judge had a very strange name. It sounded Greek, I thought. But when she opened her mouth to speak, she was very Filipino. She spoke that kind of formal English with the long words that I never come across except in college books. The Mayor's family was ranged alongside. On the opposite benches sat the family of the victim. The mother bore herself with dignity. She kept her head bowed, but she never wept.

All through the trial, she sat there. Sometimes her husband came with her. He was a sad-looking man. But most of the time, the mother came by herself. Sometimes, during the testimony, she would utter a little gasp. Then someone would stand up and offer her a glass of water. She always took it gratefully.

I myself didn't know why I wanted to listen to those things: the number of times the girl was raped. The way they tied her down. The shot in the face, at close range. What horrified me was what they did with the body afterwards. The way they drove around in a Tamaraw van, stopped at all the beer halls, showed it off, before finally dumping it by the side of the road, at Kilometer 74.

The girl must have prayed, must have reminded them of their mothers, sisters, daughters. Oh holy God, she must have wept.

She was a gift, a gift to the Mayor. Since his 50th birthday, he'd been feeling blue, the driver said. Everyone talked about it.

How do we please the Mayor? How will we find something to give him that will make him happy?

He had plenty of money, so it couldn't be that. It had to be something else, something that would restore the bloom of youth to his pallid cheeks. Fifty! That's not so old. Jaworski's still playing basketball, after all.

The chief of police suggested it first.

"*Ulol* You are fucked up, you are crazy," they told him.

But when someone broached the matter to the Mayor, he liked the idea.

So did the Mayor's nephew, his sister's boy. He liked it so much that he volunteered to choose the victim. A classmate of his at the University. She had a boyfriend; the two were always together. No problem, no problem, said the chief of police. We'll get rid of the boyfriend.

Which they did. Shooting him in the face and tossing his body down a ravine.

The girl was screaming. Her screams went up and down the scale, like a woman practicing for the opera.

Stupid. It was stupid. The nephew had never expected her to behave that way. They'd dragged her off screaming. Even in the car, they were already starting to rip off her denim shorts.

And then the numbers, the numbers, the numbers.

The numbers, the Mayor said. Today had to be the day because the numerology charts said so. It was extremely propitious.

So he sang to her first. Sinatra songs. Strangers in the Night. It Was a Very Good Year. When Somebody Loves You.

But then he grew tired of her constant sniveling. She was crouched in a corner, no shorts now, panties half-ripped.

"Tie her up," he told his men.

And then the fun began.

It was a birthday to remember. The girl's cries only increased the Mayor's pleasure. He penetrated her again and again, each time slamming her body deeper into the mattress. When he was finished, blood spattered the sheet between her legs. "Boys," he said grandly to the men standing around the bed, "take her. She is now my gift to you."

———————

The Mayor was the lord of *jueteng* in the town. Jueteng, a poor man's lotto, a numbers game. Everyday, runners took bets from the jeepney drivers, the *tiyanggi* owners, the cigarette vendors. The people gave the runners their few crumpled pesos and then waited anxiously for the results of the daily raffles. Winners were announced in the late afternoon. There was always someone who won just enough. The rest of the money, the Mayor got to keep.

He had three children. The girl was named Ave Maria. The Virgin Mary had appeared to him in a dream and given him the lucky number which was the key to all his wealth. His knees were bruised from the countless times he had made penitence by crawling to the altar from the entrance of the Calauan church. His wife, Fe, swore to all in court that her husband was with her the night the beauty queen was murdered, may she rot in hell if she were not telling the truth. In the past, it is true he may have been a little naughty, perhaps he'd even had a girlfriend on the side, but he had made his confession to a priest who had told him, *Pinapatawad ka ng Panginoong Diyos.* God forgives you. And since then he had been a paragon of devotion, going to mass with her everyday and praying the rosary.

When they came to arrest him, the men were understandably nervous. They were Laguna policemen, not from the town. When they arrived, they had been informed that the Calauan policemen had already secured a suspect, a jilted lover of the young girl. They had investigated all leads but, aside from the one suspect, no other information was forthcoming.

The town closed in on itself. The Tamaraw van where the body had been taken was washed clean. Then the woman's shorts had surfaced. Yes, the Mayor himself had turned them over to the astonished policemen, saying that a "concerned citizen" had found them on the side of the road and given them to the Mayor "for safekeeping."

Things unravel, slowly. The shorts led to other discoveries. A torn belt loop on the road leading to the Mayor's farm.

———

The Mayor was having breakfast in his *azotea*, where he liked to listen to the sounds of birds trilling in the garden. Here it was very peaceful and he could gather his thoughts before undertaking the business of the day.

It was a muggy morning in August. Rain was threatening. The maid had just poured his coffee. He was leaning forward to take a bite out of a hot *pan de sal* when he saw them, the four policemen in khaki uniforms crossing the sala. The coffee scalded his tongue just then. *Putang ina!* He hardly had time to put down the cup and wipe his lips.

He heard one of them say, "... for the murder of Mary Eileen Soria." He tried to remember what his numerology chart said.

He rose from the table. The maid screamed to see the teacup, all the breakfast things crashing to the ground.

"Señora! Señora!" she called.

The Mayor's wife came running from the bedroom, her slippers going slap, slap against the tiled floor. She was still in her house dress, her hair uncombed. Her eyes bulged. She stopped short when she saw the men.

"*Hayop ka!* Animals! How dare you–!" she screamed.

No one looked at her. The men's sweat trickled down the backs of their necks, staining the sleeves of their uniforms.

Their jeep was waiting on the driveway. A mob of angry townsfolk had surrounded it and the driver was gripping the steering wheel nervously, staring straight ahead. When the people saw the Mayor in handcuffs, an angry murmur went up. They pelted the policemen with stones. *Ang aming ama!* They cried. Our father. Don't take away our father. The Mayor was snarling now; he couldn't help it.

———————

It was the driver who cracked and ratted on the Mayor. I remember my mother mentioning this to me as she nonchalantly sprinkled water on the leaves of her orchids. The sun shone

6

behind her head, creating an aureole around her grey hair.

They'd offered the driver a chance at her, but he refused. He'd been thinking of his two little girls at home. So he only watched while they did it: the nephew, four bodyguards, the gardener, the houseboy...

———————

Inside the airless Pasig courtroom, I watched it played out: the Mayor, his bodyguards (beefy and mean-looking, just as in my dreams), his wife, the girl's mother. I had to see them all, arrayed in the courtroom, figures obscured by smoke and dim light. I had to see them, to convince myself this was real, it had really happened. It wasn't a nightmare. That this, everything I had been told, was not just some figment of my imagination, but had actually happened, in that town.

———————

Sometimes, because I'd lived apart so long, I couldn't quite be sure of who I was. There were letters, of course, letters from back home. The letters told me nothing of who I was or who I had been. They were always filled with details of birthday parties, weddings, births, and funerals. None of these occasions affected me personally. I felt like someone looking at fish swimming around in a fishbowl.

When I went to the courtroom, I had this idea: that if I could feel hate, if I could feel that pure emotion burning up my body, then I would know where I belonged.

I didn't have any reason to be there. I was on vacation. I should have been sunning myself by the pool in my mother's backyard. Languid, I should have been languid. My arm outstretched for a cool, tall glass of *calamansi* juice. I would feel the weight in my hand–that coolness. Perhaps I'd press the glass to my hot cheek and let the drops of moisture creep down my chin.

But I couldn't be that way. There was something tearing up my insides. And every time I thought of the girl, tied down on the Mayor's *narra* bed with her legs spread-eagled, I couldn't think. I'd have to stop whatever I was doing–yes, even stop walking, even if I were in the middle of a busy intersection–and take a few deep breaths.

———————

The Mayor's men were holding her arms so tight, so tight. She couldn't breathe. *Turbohin na rin natin ang tinurbo ni Boss,* she heard one of them say. She had had seven of them already, and between her legs was a gaping wound where the milky semen leaked and leaked. Yet they were laughing and calling her names now. Cunt. Bitch.

In the morning, before leaving for school, she had handed her mother a *gumamela* from the garden. Her mother's smile...

O sige na, her mother had said. Go on; you'll be late. Her mother hadn't been feeling well. As soon as her daughter had closed the door to the bedroom, she'd turned toward the sunlight filtering through the window and fallen back asleep.

Paolo was waiting for her in his car. They always rode to school together now. Since the night of the *Santacruzan,* when she had been Reyna Elena, holding a miniature cross in her arms, he'd always wanted to be by her side. She didn't mind what the *colegialas* said, that Paolo liked girls, that he was a flirt. *Selos lang sila,* she thought. Because he's with me, not with them.

When they saw the police car at the side of the road, they didn't think anything of it, but then the policeman walked right out into the middle of the street and Paolo had to stop. Then, suddenly, there were men at either side of the car, yanking open the doors. She was thrown into the back of a van, a firm hand covering her mouth, another holding her wrists. She twisted and kicked. From the window of the van she could see the men hitting Paolo, whose head was already bloody. She bit at the hand covering her mouth and screamed. She wouldn't stop, not even after she felt the hand bruising her cheek, trying clumsily to hold her lips together. The next time she was able to look out the window she couldn't see him, couldn't see Paolo. There was a trail of blood leading to the side of the road.

Tears sprang to her eyes. She was suddenly helpless and small. She was the little girl hiding behind the *santan* flowers, the one whom everyone was looking for because she had been throwing stones at the kittens. She was the little girl hiding in the closet because her mother was angry at her for using up the perfume that was in the cut-glass bottle on her mother's night table. She had been naughty; she shouldn't have worn shorts that day. She could feel fingers at the edges of her shorts, straining toward her crotch. Hard fingers, with nails that scratched. But she didn't want to die, so maybe she should just lie very, very still. If she lay still, the fingers might stop pushing so much, and it would hurt less. Would that help? No, it didn't help. So she continued her writhing.

Paolo was nowhere now and all she wanted to do was to live. She recognized the house where they took her. And she thought: so it's true, all those stories about the Mayor.

He was the one who had put the crown on her head at the *Santacruzan* procession. He'd been there with his wife, his children. He'd smiled at her. The parish priest, Father Antonio, had clapped him on the shoulder.

———————

After he'd done it, after he was through, she relaxed a little. The Mayor had let out a small grunt of contentment and let his body sag onto hers. She rested, in that moment. She thought, now he will let me go. I've survived. But she didn't realize he would hand her over to the others, the others who'd been watching

9

at the sides of the room. His nephew, first. She recognized him from school. She screamed. He was worse than the Mayor; she couldn't bear the tearing pain between her legs.

After the nephew, they dragged her out to the van. Pulling her along, while she stumbled and slipped on the gravel in the driveway. They didn't even allow her to put her clothes back on. The servants could see her, dressed only in a T-shirt which barely reached her hips, could clearly see the bruises, the blood streaking her inner thighs.

Even after she'd had seven of them, she still wanted to live. She managed to get up, get on her knees. Supplicating, her hands together as if she'd been praying to the Virgin in the Calauan church. She said, Have mercy. A hand covered her eyes. Oh, God. She screamed this time: Have mercy! But she knew. She didn't want to open her eyes, even though the hand was gone. The gun blast hit her in the face and spattered her brains over the floor of the van.

In the courtroom, I began to notice a veiled figure who appeared every day, always in the same place. She was slender; she wore a light blue dress. Over her face was the lace veil that I remembered wearing to Church before Vatican II did away with the rule about covering one's head. I never saw this woman's face, only the merest outline of her profile. The more I saw her, the more I wanted to find out who she was.

She spoke to no one. She always sat demurely, her hands folded on her lap. After many weeks, I began to get the feeling that she was the mystery girl. I thought her hands, with their faint tracery of blue veins, looked very familiar.

When I asked people who she was, they would shrug, because no one had noticed her particularly. There were so many spectators in that courtroom, it was actually difficult to breathe. There were days when the smell of human sweat, and all the tension collected in people's bodies, was so overpowering that I literally kept a handkerchief to my nose the whole time I sat there.

I didn't want to be there and yet I was there.

When it was all, all over, when the Mayor was being taken away in handcuffs, when his wife was wailing and gnashing her teeth, when the flashbulbs were popping and there was general pandemonium, desks toppling over and people scuffling to be the first to get the story out, I couldn't move. People shoved me from behind, cursing. They were trying to get to the girl's mother.

"What do you think about the verdict?" they asked her. "Are you happy?"

That was the first time I saw the woman's eyes fill with tears. She didn't answer, only pushed her way wordlessly out of the room.

Much, much later, when I was myself again, I opened a newspaper and there was his picture. I couldn't mistake that shock of hair that looked like a rug, those pig eyes. He was sitting in a bathtub, and, from what I could see of him, was apparently naked. The caption said that the picture had been taken in jail. But the Mayor was smiling. The article said the Mayor's bath water was sprinkled with rose petals provided by his loving wife, Fe, the new Mayor of Calauan.

RUFINO

*Towards the end, he couldn't wear any clothes. They had
to cover him in banana leaves.*

It was in July he died – I couldn't believe it. A voice on
the phone told me.

"Rufino died *na.*" It was my mother speaking. Naturally,
she had to be the one to break the news.

I was staying in a friend's house in the Santa Cruz Mountains.
In the mornings, fog blanketed the hills. We heard the mournful
mooing of invisible cows. One or another of us would look east,
toward where we heard Neil Young had his ranch, wondering
whether we'd catch a glimpse of his pink Cadillac that day.

At night we made a fire and played Scrabble. We drank hot
chocolate and felt like teenagers having a slumber party. Our
husbands were both out of town on business. Though with my
husband, I could never really be sure. Sometimes one friend
or another would say, "I saw your husband at such-and-such
a place," and it would be somewhere else from where he told
me he would be.

We used to joke about it. Once, my friend was in a grocery,
and she heard the cashier say, "Call R___. This lady needs help
with her groceries." And since R___ is my husband's name, we
both fell over laughing at the memory, at the thought that my
husband might actually show up, in a Safeway uniform, to bag
my friend's groceries. But there was a thread of sadness in my
life, too, at that moment.

Our children were away together at a summer camp in Clear
Lake, up north. We were at an easy time in our lives.

Once I saw a coyote crossing the path in front of me. It was
my first coyote. Such a skinny little thing, almost nothing but
a bag of bones. With long, pointed ears. It looked at me and

13

then lost interest. It loped along into the tall grass. I wanted to call it back, to give it a name.

––––––––––

When my mother told me about Rufino, I put my head down on the table where the telephone rested. The wood felt cool against my forehead.

"*Ay*, it was his time *na*," my mother kept saying.

The last time I saw him, he was a face at a window. I was standing by our swimming pool, gazing down at the water which was then filled with brown leaves from a heavy rainfall, ended just moments earlier. I don't know why I was standing there by myself that afternoon. Something glinted in the water, made me look up. The window looked out over our backyard. There, in a tiny room off our kitchen, I saw him. The window had grills. He looked like a prisoner, with his sad face.

He wasn't wearing any clothes and when he saw me looking at him he hunched over instinctively. I saw his skinny back, the ribs protruding through the skin, which was paler than I remembered.

The face I saw was the same as the one I remembered from the time I'd left home, twenty years ago. I stood, transfixed. His gaze was piercing.

I was no longer a young girl. There was gray in my hair. Rufino and I looked at each other. We didn't speak. Finally he put one hand up to his face, as if ashamed. I looked away, wanting to grant him his privacy, remembering how proud he used to be.

––––––––––

He was the family driver for almost 20 years. He came to us when I was five. I don't remember how it happened: perhaps he'd heard my parents were looking for a driver. Perhaps he walked up the driveway of the house in Carolina Street, the house I think we lived in, though now my mother tells me we never lived there. She told me this only a few months ago, while chattering away about something. Oh? I said. So we never lived in Malate, in that small street behind the Baclaran Church? No, never, she said.

And that is why I have to call this fiction. Because I am not sure anymore what to call the images that spring up in my mind. Whether it is of my husband, or of my memories of my childhood home—nothing is fixed, everything changes.

The image I have of the house is of a tall iron gate, rusting, and a large sampaguita tree, fragrant with white flowers. I may have been playing outside with my sister and the *yaya* when he walked up the driveway. Whoever saw him first would have had to stop and stare. He was unbelievably handsome: as handsome as those early Don Johnson photos, the kind of handsome that I could see would drive the 14-year-old Melanie Griffiths wild.

My mother always responded to people with looks. I didn't realize this until much, much later, when she told me she thought I should have my nose fixed. She hired Rufino on the spot, even before he'd offered his references.

He was never happy, even after my father paid for a correspondence course so that he could get a degree in mechanics. He always quarreled with one or the other of the maids. He slept with the cook, Clarita. The laundry-woman, Vangeline, he chased with a knife. Once we came home and found him with his hands around the *mayordoma's* throat. Pandemonium greeted us. Of course he did not kill the *mayordoma.* And he continued driving for us, as before.

I was not sure why Rufino hated the *mayordoma.* She was a big woman, with unnaturally white skin. The others said she was the daughter of a *tulisan,* a bandit. She was nearly six feet tall, an aberration in our country. And with that white skin, even after growing up dirt poor in the provinces, the others thought she was strange.

Rufino and the *mayordoma* often had arguments in the kitchen. We would hear their voices rising, fierce, while we sat in the dining room and tried to make small talk with whoever happened to be visiting us that day. My father would ring the bell. *"Hipus da!"* he would shout, his face getting red. We learned to pass the dinner plates with one ear cocked towards the kitchen.

He had a Kawasaki motorcycle my father had given him. I used to watch him in the garage, endlessly oiling its various gears.

A smell rose off him—a pungent smell, like garlic. My mother gave him bars of imported soap to wash with. Impossible to remove this smell, however. It was as much a part of him as the air he breathed.

Why did my mother like him so much?

Was it because he drove fast, faster than any of the other drivers she tried, and he looked good, too, standing and waiting for her beside the car.

In the years after his stroke, he lived first in a little shanty next to his sister's hut, in one of the far-flung slums of Manila. Then my mother rescued him and he lived above the garage. On all my visits home, every two or three years, he was a shadowy presence. I knew he was there, but I never saw him.

Sometimes, coming home late at night, I would see a light on in the little room. I would look at the shuttered windows and think of him. But I would pass on into the house and forget that he was there, that I had even thought of him.

16

And so the years passed, and one year I came home with my son, who was two. What joy, what happiness there was in the house! Everyone made much of him, because he was the first grandchild. After that, he came every other year: when he was four, when he was six, eight, ten.

When he was six, he knew about Rufino, the man who lived above the garage. I explained to him that Rufino was a member of our family: our driver since I was five years old, since we lived in the little house in Malate. My son knew, and would often ask about him. But he never saw him.

I alone saw him that day. Standing in the garden, a middle-aged woman, gray in my hair, looking down at the swimming pool that my mother was using to raise fish. Mosquitoes hovered over the murky water. I saw the black darting shapes of the fish. I saw the nets bundled up by the pool steps. I saw him look at me and thought: *does he know who I am?*

His eyes were startled but aware. All these years, I had formed a picture in my mind of a wreck, someone I wouldn't recognize. My mother had told me, don't try to see him, it will only make you sad. So, sitting in the kitchen with Rona, his wife, I would give her pictures of my son to take to him.

I trusted my mother so completely. It seemed to me that if she said I would be horrified, it would be true. When I saw him that day in the garden, for the first time I began to doubt my mother's words. But I was already old.

When my mother told me he had died, I didn't at first think of the succession of houses we had moved to, with him. A year later, they came back to me.

There was the Bel-Air house, when I was very little. My brothers were born there; I was already five. Then we moved to Dasmariñas. I was nine. Here was where the cook, Clarita, came running to my father with tears in her eyes, complaining that Rufino had grabbed her breasts. A month later she went back to her home in Bacolod. Rufino stayed.

Then there was Paraiso. We moved there when I was 17. I had a boyfriend then. His name was Mon. That year, Mon and I stayed all the time in the den, with the blinds drawn, kissing.

Those months with Mon, Rufino was always cleaning the pool, just outside the den. Mon and I would close the blinds. He'd knock on the sliding glass doors, wanting something. I wanted him to go away, disappear. He always came knocking. He'd say, your mother wants you. Or, your father's home.

Rona became our cook. She would glower at Rufino each time he honked on the horn for someone to open the gate. One day I came running back to the house alone, after everyone had gone to mass, because I'd forgotten something. I knocked and knocked on Rona's door. "Please, please!" I shouted. Rufino pulled it open. He was bare-chested, and I saw the sweat streaming down his neck. He was panting. Behind him, I saw the rumbled bed. I didn't see Rona, but I knew she was there. The air coming from the room was hot and acrid. I knew what had been going on there, though I didn't say a word. I turned and joined the others at mass. I kept silent.

When Rona became pregnant, my parents had had enough. You must marry her, they told Rufino. He didn't want to, but they made him.

Rona was ugly. She was old. She was nothing like Clarita. Her skin was dark, and already wrinkled. But still, that's who Rufino married.

———

And maybe it would have been better if the story ended here, but it doesn't. Perhaps he should have buckled down, become a docile husband and father, happy to be in service and to have a roof over his head. As long he could drive for us, his future was secure. What more could anyone want, especially

18

someone who started out with nothing?

They lived with us, and had a child. Violeta, they named her. She was a big girl, who in form reminded me a little of the *mayordoma* whom Rufino had once throttled over the kitchen sink. That is, she had broad, burly shoulders, like a man. Even when she was 12, she had that heftiness.

She played with my son, on our visits home. At that time, the pool hadn't yet been turned into a fishpond. She put him in a rubber tire and floated him lazily from one end of the pool to the other, back and forth like that, all afternoon. She was too shy to put on a bathing suit. She went into the water fully clothed, her skirt billowing around her. From the upstairs bedroom I heard my son's delighted shouts. She never bothered to put swimming trunks on him. I saw his little brown body, wriggling in the center of the black tire. Violeta's black hair, streaming behind her, and the red skirt which she wore day after day, floating around them like a cape.

Because I had fond memories of Violeta and my son playing in the pool, I could hardly believe it when, later, my mother told me this same Violeta would shout and even strike Rufino. After his stroke, he couldn't move, he was helpless. It fell to Violeta to feed him his meals, while her mother was busy serving us. It was a job Violeta hated with a passion, hated the idea of having to spoon the rice gruel into this old man's mouth, and having to wipe off the drool that spilled out at the corners. When Rona became old and weak, it became Violeta's job to turn Rufino on the bed, so he would not get bedsores. But still, by the time he died, his body was covered with them.

———————

I remember calling home, a few weeks before Rufino died. Rona answered the phone.

She said, "*Ay, 'day*, Rufino's very sick. But it's no use calling the doctor. It's his time."

19

He'd had his stroke just after I'd gone to the States to live. He was partially paralyzed now and lived all the time in that little room. He had to be fed and bathed and was always urinating on himself. My mother said Rona was tired. Rona was worn out, taking care of him.

I asked Rona, "Who is taking care of him now?" She said, "Violeta." I thought of Violeta sitting around all day in the kitchen, watching soaps on the little black-and-white TV my mother had put there.

"Can she take care of him?" I asked.

"No, 'day, it is very hard for her. She can't even lift him. So his back is covered with sores."

I was upset. I knew Violeta was a strapping girl, and Rufino was so thin. "Well, *she has to lift him.* Do you hear me? Tell her she has to do it. What is the number at your place?"

Almost the same moment I asked the question, I remembered. So I said, "Do you have a phone?"

"No, 'day," she said. "But my next door neighbor has one."

I knew Rona lived very far away, in the outer reaches of Manila, and it took her a long time to get home on her days off, so that in the past couple of years she had stopped going home every weekend, and my mother thought it a kindness to move Rufino to our house. These outer regions of the city were mysterious to me–as mysterious as any unexplored country. I imagined Rona riding in a succession of buses and jeepneys; the last leg of the journey a pedicab ride. The houses in this area would be small; yet they were a cut above squatters' shanties. They might be situated next to an *estero*, an open canal. But TV antennas and satellite dishes sprouted like mushrooms on the rickety tin roofs. And the children ran around in Nikes and Reeboks, sent by relatives working in Saudi Arabia or Kuwait.

Now Rona told me she had brought Rufino back there, to her house. But I know he hated it there. He only wanted to be close to us, his other family. Once, my brother told me, Rufino had come to our subdivision. It had probably taken him days of

20

walking. The guard at the gate had stopped him and wouldn't let him pass because he smelled of urine. The guard called our house, and my brother went to fetch him.

His pants stank. It seemed he hadn't washed for days. That was why my mother had finally made a little room for him, near the kitchen.

"When did you bring him home?" I asked.

Last week, Rona said. Then she said, "Let him go, 'day. He is no use to anybody now."

That evening I e-mailed my brother. He lived in a suburb of Manila, close to my mother.

Will you please, please see to it that Rufino has a doctor, I wrote. Rona tells me he is dying and she is not prepared to do anything about it.

I kept e-mailing him, and there was no reply.

Weeks passed and I thought, perhaps Rona is only imagining it. Perhaps Rufino is not dying. Sometimes, because I lived so far from home, it was easy for me to tell myself that things I heard were not true, were not really happening. My mother would call to complain about one of my brothers. I would listen for a while, but by the time I hung up the phone I had forgotten most of what she said.

Then, one night, I got a call from my mother. We talked about various things. She told me about a dream she'd had: she'd seen an orderly entering a house, the house of one of my uncles, who later died. Sometimes her stories could still surprise me. Oh, when was this, I asked. Last November, she said. And oh, she added, almost as an afterthought, Rufino died *na*.

The *na* was what convinced me it was real. We put this small word at the end of many of our sentences. It implies fulfillment. Something waited for. Not waited for fervently, but patiently, with expectation that the inevitable will happen. The only question is when. When the inevitable does happen, we say it happened *na*. We are like this, we Filipinos.

My mother had already begun to talk about something else. She had said it so quickly, almost as casually as if she

21

had blinked an eye. If I were not listening so carefully, I might have missed it.

She continued to talk, but I pressed my head against the wall. I felt terrible. I couldn't speak.

Finally, impatient because I was so silent, and because she was calling long-distance, she said, "Well, I better go."

"Yes," I said, and added nothing more. Suddenly, I was ashamed of my inexplicable access of grief for our old driver.

My brother e-mailed me a week later. He wrote, Don't feel bad. Rufino was not the same after his stroke. He went downhill so quickly.

"Did you attend the funeral?" I asked.

No, no one had.

And perhaps it was too much to expect—that one of the children would have gone to that out-of-the-way mortuary or chapel, perhaps somewhere in the provinces, where Rufino's relatives would have taken his body.

He added, "Did you see Tito Mario when he was there? I went to his house last night and he talked about seeing Paolo and Maia, I thought they'd split up but I guess they're back together again..."

It is many years later and my son is about to graduate from high school. I overhear a conversation he is having with a friend. They're in my son's room, the two boys lounging on throw pillows on the floor. My son says, "We used to have a man in a cage in our house in Manila." The other boy snorts. He knows my son's fondness for telling stories.

22

"It's true," my son says. "We kept him caged up, like an animal."

I think—this is Rufino he is talking about. *Rufino.*

I put my hand on the door.

But the boys have moved on. They are talking about some video game now. Something about "levels" and "extra life." I don't understand.

We kept Rufino with us because we wanted to be kind. The little room he was in had barred windows, that part was true. There was a wooden stool by the window on which he used to sit. There was a thin mattress and a bedpan. The floor was cement. The walls were bare. If he listened, he could hear his daughter humming the latest Martin Nievera hit in the kitchen. He could hear hurried footsteps. People running and fetching. Shouts and murmurs. Life.

Staring out, perhaps he did look like some animal, like some caged beast that is waiting, only waiting, for the final metamorphosis.

OAKS

I

The truth is, everything she did these days was what her family might call "unbalanced."

For instance, she'd visited her husband once at his officemate's apartment. The officemate was named Dan. She had never met him, but she looked up his address from a company roster her husband had left behind. The apartment was in a complex called The Oaks, near the San Jose Airport. There were no trees anywhere; she wondered how the complex had gotten its name. Perhaps there had been, at one time, large trees where the apartments were now. But they'd apparently been cut down, every single one of them. Perhaps they'd even been victims of sudden oak death, which she knew had been a problem mentioned in the newspapers—on the rare occasions when she happened to read them—recently. All she had seen, that one time she visited, were low buildings and rows of small Japanese cars–Honda, Toyota, Nissan—parked in numbered spaces by the building entrances.

She'd never been to this part of San Jose before. In fact, she rarely ventured south, disliking the monotony of the buildings, the featureless streets. This part of the Bay Area felt different, flatter. The buildings were makeshift, thrown together. The freeway was close by and she could hear the roar of traffic.

Somewhere, she thought, there must be houses, with fences, trees, yards. But they were behind sound walls, out of sight.

She thought of her husband driving a different way to work now—not over the Dumbarton Bridge, as before, but south, through San Jose. She'd traced his route on a map. Brokaw Road east to 880, then north. He'd have to pass Milpitas and the Great Mall, the place she'd caught them having lunch together. That day seemed so long ago now, another lifetime, but she realized suddenly that it had only been a month.

She was afraid she would have to make some sort of explanation to Dan, but it was Vic himself who'd opened the door. Perhaps

25

Dan had spied her through the peephole and called Vic. At any rate, her husband was looking at her now, with his familiar look of exasperation.

She noticed everything about him: the fine, soft, fawn-colored shirt, one he'd worn only on meeting days, and dark gray pants. What she thought of as his "dressing up clothes."

"What do you want?" he said right away. He seemed to be in a hurry, his hand on the doorknob, as if getting ready to close the door on her.

"Nothing," she said. "I just wanted to drop by."

"Look, this is not a good time," he said. "I was getting ready to go someplace. I have to meet—someone."

She looked at him. He read the question in her eyes and chose not to answer it.

"Next time, call first," he said.

"Well, I was in the area..." she lied. "I thought you might want to have lunch."

"I can't, I'm busy," he repeated.

His new life. What does he want? Not even Selena, really. He wants her friendship, it means a lot to him, but not anything more than that.

All their married life she'd known him to dole out pieces of himself sparingly—even the sex. He'd always delighted in foreplay, quickly losing interest during the act itself. From the way he talked so glowingly of the younger woman, Malou knew they'd never slept together.

And Selena—Malou knew she didn't want anything more because she, too, had a family. But for this friendship with the younger woman her husband was willing to leave her, their son, and their life of 15 years together.

She looked, now, at his hands. *I never liked them before, he always kept his nails too long.* Now she imagined some other woman looking, too, and liking what she saw. They were smooth, supple hands, the skin paler than the rest of him.

"Can't you see your friends some other time?" she asked. "I came all this way—"

She saw him hesitate. Then, quickly, he made up his mind. "Wait here," he said.

26

He turned his back on her and closed the door. In a very short time, he was back, shrugging on a leather jacket. She wondered if he'd spoken to someone inside. Dan? Or had he made a phone call? What she'd seen of the room behind him was spartan and neat. A man's room. There was a sofa, two love seats, a large-screen TV, a glass-topped coffee table. A magazine—*Car & Driver,* she thought—lay flipped open on the table, next to an open bottle of Pacifico.

"What have you been up to?" she asked him as they walked to his car. She was alarmed at the sudden catch in her voice. It was a bright, sunny day. Her heels seemed to stick on the freshly laid asphalt. The tears stung her eyes. She saw he was still driving the same old Honda. He'd parked at the back of the complex, in a spot she had never thought to look, on the days she'd swung by.

"Work," he said.

"Are you happy?" she asked him, then.

"Not entirely," he said. "But it's a start." He paused. "I probably won't be here long."

"What are you planning to do?" she asked.

"I don't know," he said. She noted the nonchalance in his voice. *This is new.* "Maybe find my own place. Nearer the office."

"Johnmel misses you," she said.

For the first time, she saw something—an emotion—flicker across his face. But he said smoothly, "I'll drop by and visit him this weekend."

"You will—?" she said, hopefully, and was about to continue when he cut her off.

"But I can't be long. I have to meet Selena."

"Oh?" she asked. "What for? A party?"

He made a face. Her asking about Selena seemed to physically pain him. But she had to. And he, too, strove for a kind of honesty for he always answered her.

"She's graduating," he said. "She got her degree."

"That's nice," she said.

She remembered how he'd gotten the company to pay for her education, two years ago now. She realizes suddenly, *that was when it all began.*

"Will Mike be going?" she asked. Mike, the chairman of the company, who'd been so nice to her before, before all this.

"I don't know," he said. "Maybe."

She began to sense a rising impatience. He turned into a parking lot. "We're here," he said.

It turned out to be Goldilocks. She was disappointed. When he meant a quick lunch, he wasn't exaggerating.

They went inside. The tables were full of people, all talking and laughing together. No one glanced at them as they made their way across the room. She noticed that there were a few very pretty young women—slim, with luxuriant black hair and alluring smiles. She thought regretfully, *I should have dressed up a bit more.*

He handed her a tray and she pointed at the dishes displayed behind the counter: *pansit*, and some *adobo* with rice. He selected a *siopao*.

"Is that all you're having?" she asked. "Are you on a diet?"

"I am not on a diet," he said testily. "I'm just not hungry."

As soon as they were seated, his hand wandered to his pocket and he pulled out his cell phone. After checking the display, he stood up. "I'll just be a minute," he said. Without waiting for a response, he walked outside.

Through the glass, she watched him. He was talking to someone. They were good friends, judging from the expression on her husband's face. He didn't hurry back. He paced back and forth, head down, talking on the phone. She waited five, 10, 15 minutes. Finally, she began to eat. After she had taken a couple of mouthfuls, he came back to the table.

They ate quickly. Neither of them had much to say. She wanted to ask about the phone call, but she knew he wouldn't tell her who it really was. He would lie, and the lie would hurt just as much as the truth. He had never spent so much time talking to her on the phone, even when they were first married. Perhaps she should have known, back then. Known about his lack of commitment.

And yet, their marriage had lasted 15 years. How was it possible for two people to remain together that long, without being in love?

It had all started with his friendship with Dan. Dan was 35, 10 years younger than Vic. He'd joined the company a year after Vic, and they started having drinks after work.

Then Dan got a divorce. He began to talk to Vic about his dates. Rightly or wrongly, she blamed Dan for Vic's starting with Selena. Dan probably encouraged him, egged him on. Convinced him it was nothing. Just an office flirtation, Dan probably said. He probably told Vic, "She likes you, man! Go ahead and have a little fun!"

Dan had a band. They played 80s music. Vic went to bars to listen to Dan's band, leaving Malou at home.

He doesn't really know what he wants.

And what about us—Johnmel and I? We are all alone. We hardly talk to each other anymore. When he comes home from school, he dumps his knapsack by the door, goes to his room and closes the door.

She took a breath.

"Can't you," she began. "Can't you—just—come home?"

"No!" he said. His fame assumed a stubborn, closed look. Strangely, she felt love, leaping in her chest. Even as he pulled away.

The tears jumped to her eyes, she couldn't help it.

"Look," he said, more gently. "I know you think this is about her, but it's not."

"Then what *is* it about?" she asked.

"I have to start over," he said. "I need a new life."

She is somewhat envious, now. That her husband has decided to take control of his own happiness.

II

She looked back at the building, but he'd gone inside and she couldn't tell whether he was watching her or not. She thought, *this is an ugly place.* And by "this" she didn't only mean The Oaks, but the whole of the Valley, with its scrawny little saplings planted

29

in concrete boxes before the glass buildings. And she loathed the people in the buildings, too, shut off from everything in their glass boxes, intently poring over the numbers for the technology that they hoped would carry the Valley to its next boom. In the last few years, all her husband had talked about was making money, putting down enough for a vacation home in Lake Tahoe, getting himself a BMW.

I should have known, she thought. *I should have known.*

Impulsively, she walked up to his car. She still had the spare key. She stuck it in the lock and yanked open the driver's door.

She looked around. Neat as a pin. Nothing under the seats. The six-year-old upholstery was spotless. She inhaled deeply, trying to catch his scent, and perhaps the scent of someone new. She was suddenly seized with a powerful curiosity to imagine who could be sitting next to him when he drove to lunch, when he left work for the day.

Selena, she knew, was Vietnamese. She dressed well. She had beautiful hair and skin, and large, dark eyes. Now Malou would find herself looking at women she passed on the street, trying to tell whether they were Vietnamese or not. The few Vietnamese women she'd known had a powerful femininity. Small hands and feet. Pale skin. They were delicate, but with surprisingly harsh voices. They seemed to possess a core of steel, beneath the fluttery movements.

She sat behind the wheel and absent-mindedly reached into the glove compartment. She pulled out a pack of cigarettes, a box of matches—when had he started smoking? She turned over the matchbox: a blonde woman in a cowboy outfit was on the cover. A balloon next to the woman's mouth said: "Until I find a real man, I'll take a real smoke." Written in pencil next to that, in her husband's familiar hand, were the words, "No bull."

Malou rested her forehead on the steering wheel; she was suddenly very tired.

III

Malou lay sleepless on the bed. Her mother and she had exchanged words. Her mother had said, "You did what? Why'd you do a crazy thing like that for? Leave him alone, you can't do anything about him anyway! You're acting like a lovesick teenager!" Malou had cried. She thought her mother was right. She thought that perhaps this was why Vic had left her.

She lay awake, thinking of her husband in Dan's apartment, in the complex named after the dead trees. She imagined the two men watching ESPN–her husband was always a sports buff. They were probably drinking Pacifico and talking about the office. She knew they'd never talk about her. If they talked about anyone at all it would be about the young Vietnamese woman with the sad eyes, the woman whose pictures her husband carried around in his wallet.

She turned on her side. Tonight Johnmel had told her he might want to drop out of school for a year.

"To do what?" she asked.

He shrugged. "Maybe I'll stay with *lola* in the Philippines," he said.

Malou looked at him. "You never liked the food there," she said.

"Maybe I'll get used to it," he said.

He is only 13, she thought. But in his eyes there was a strange determination, and in the last year–she couldn't be imagining this–the down had darkened over his upper lip and he looked, at certain angles, like a man she didn't know.

She sighed. The window was open, and outside she could hear the night, the soft breath of wind in the bushes. It calmed her. She thought, she prayed, that Johnmel would be all right. That her husband, in the apartment miles south, would find happiness. She prayed fervently, her eyes shut, without even knowing that she was praying. Her lips moved involuntarily, sometimes saying her husband's name. She didn't sense Johnmel's presence, watching from the doorway.

The boy felt pity and also a kind of hatred for the woman praying on the bed. He would have liked to reach out to her, but the hatred was stronger now and he turned and headed back to his room, a shadow moving down the silent hallway.

AMERICAN MILK

There's nothing we can do.

The line stares up at me. It is from a novel which I am reading in my office when I know I am supposed to be working on this year's grant budget. Strangely, reading it restores my concentration and I begin filing papers, knowing exactly where each one will go without the usual doubts and hesitations. June expense statements go into a large red binder, clipped to the month's invoices. I have filed everything properly under either "Supplies" or "Maintenance." The whole operation has taken me just 20 minutes.

I take another peek at the book.

In six months she will be going to London to do research ...

Ah! This gives me pause. I stare at the palm trees outside, at the birds–could they be swallows? Suddenly, I realize I do not know what a swallow looks like. In the Philippines, we had little brown birds called maya birds that perched on the telephone wires strung up and down the street in front of our house. They were ugly little birds but they were the only kind I saw and I knew without a doubt that they could not be anything like the swallows I read about in books.

For the last ten years, I have lived in California. Here people seem to like nature very much. Californians talk endlessly about the environment, about the joys of hiking in a national park with a backpack, heavy boots, and a portable stove. But I grew up in the Philippines, home of the denuded tropical rain forests, the illegal strip miners, the lahar-spewing volcanoes, the off-the-scale pollution index.

So I have never liked nature. And I don't understand the nature here; or, at least, the nature as it exists in California: the dry, dry ground; the giant palm trees with their fat trunks that line Palm Drive in Stanford University, where I work as a Title VI grant administrator; the neatly clipped lawns; the giant

33

flowers whose names I do not know.

I am oriented towards aspects of the weather: whether it is raining or not raining; whether it is cold one day and not so cold the next day; whether the sky is blue or gray. These are the limits of my observations about nature.

P. 45: Of course, he is in very good shape, and very well muscled ...

Which leads me to think of my dear hubby, hard at work in his office in the Palo Alto hills. We have been married almost eight years. In those years, his face has grown considerably rounder, and his waist has developed little bumps of flesh on each side that, I found out from an American joke book I was browsing through one day, can euphemistically be referred to as love handles. His hair is turning gray, and the expression on his face when he looks at me now holds traces of uncertainty. I cannot, by any stretch of the imagination, consider him "well muscled" or even "fit".

P. 47: "We'll take it," says Mrs. Bush unexpectedly.

What do I make of this line? I read it in the car, at a stoplight, on my way home from work. I have chosen to take the Alameda de las Pulgas, which is extremely winding, and has stop signs at every intersection. My six-year-old son is in the back seat, talking about Game Gear.

Take what? Just like that? Is this something I should practice saying? To the other mothers at my son's private school, perhaps? With my head tilted back, my lips curled? Perhaps I should blow-dry my hair? Have a manicure/pedicure? What IS this line trying to tell me? Inside I know it's not the words themselves but the confidence behind the words, uttered with simplicity and directness, that I lack ...

"Mrs. Bush, I'd like you to meet ..."

I have listened to variations of this introduction, usually at social functions at my son's school: the formal address coupled with the extending of the hand, the slightly abstract gaze. Now I become so agitated I lose my concentration and nearly crash into the car in front of me. My son protests that my driving has caused him to push his See's lollipop, a present from his teacher, almost all the way into the back of his throat. My husband says that ever since my son's accident with a New York subway token when he was one and a half, my son does not have an easy time swallowing food, which perhaps accounts for the fact that, at six, he is only 41 lbs.

P. 48: As soon as Lois says this ...

Says what? Like the unfortunate Lois, I am always saying things that cause me to feel defensive afterwards. Is this woman, who in this story has inherited a huge brownstone from "a legacy," perhaps more like me than was initially apparent? I am excited and plunge on madly, my eyes darting right and left, my foot on the accelerator.

Charles could willingly clobber Lois ...

This I read at home, on the bed, while my son sits in his dirty play clothes in front of the television set. (Bad mother, bad mother!)

"When you want me to take Geraldine ," says Charles ...

Who is Geraldine? A dog! Only a dog! I immediately remember my son, abandoned in front of the television set. I jump up and sing, "Time for a bath! Time for a bath!"

Customary protests. Kicks. I feel defeated, remembering that when I was growing up in Manila, no one I knew–child or adult–exhibited this particular form of behavior. While I am shouting in my best drill-sergeant imitation, I am wondering whether my son is this way because he has lived six years in America, or because he is an only child, or because I am an unfit mother, or because he has had a hard day in first grade. All these thoughts run through my head while I maneuver him into the bathroom and out of his clothes, which smell pungently of sweat and caked earth.

Throughout the tumult preceding her divorce, she never gave him the satisfaction ...

This line gives me the opportunity to be smug. But I am also, strangely, depressed. My dear hubby pops into my head again. How many times have I given him the satisfaction ...

Now she screams ...

Oh, oh, oh. This is wicked. This is tempting.

She forgets that she planned to abandon Charles ...

Serves you right! Bitch! You're 44, you have a 28-year-old lover, and you complain! Paradoxically, I am also filled with remorse, and I immediately jump up and begin clearing this morning's dishes from the sink. I do it quickly, before the desire flags. I also toss clothes into the washing machine and, while I'm at it, spritz water on the house plants.

He will never seem more desirable than he does now ...

I must remind myself to be nicer to poor hubby. Prepare home-cooked meals, not keep writing bad things about him in my diary. My last entry about him reads: PIG! PIG! PIG!

She has been weeding in her garden when he suddenly appears ...

Perhaps I should busy myself with something constructive, instead of lying on the bed reading a book! I begin to whip up a chicken curry dish that I'd been planning to make for the last three days. There is much chopping to be done: green peppers, onions, garlic, apples, tomatoes. I toss everything into the Cuisinart, but afterwards my energy flags and I decide to finish the rest of the steps at some other time. Back to the book, and–

He gardens sporadically ...

I decide to take a peek at the front lawn. My husband has agonized over this lawn all summer. He stands on the dry brown grass with a hose for close to an hour every day. Yet the grass is no greener, and a few of the flowers we planted only last week are already shriveled up, their leaves crackly and colorless.

Nevertheless she steps through the ilex ...

Aha! The woman has met someone! Her defenses have been breached! She is about to have an Affair!

Because he is a writer ...

My disappointment is keen. It seems to me that the author is copping out. To have an affair with a writer seems almost too convenient. The affair I can swallow, but definitely not the writer part. This is simply asking for too much. If the affair had been with a car salesman or a computer engineer or even a professor ...

My faith in the narrator shaken, I decide to return the book to the library the next morning.

I've never seen ...

I am beginning to lose my concentration.

Depressed in advance ...

Yes, this describes my mood perfectly.

If it's morality you want ...

And why, I ask myself, do I never have occasion to say something as witty and sparkling as this to any of my next door neighbors?

The last line I read of the book:

May Mildred be smashed with heavy thesauruses, smitten with semi-colons.

———————

In the morning I drop my son off at school, pleased because I have made it before morning prayers. He clambers reluctantly out of the car. On the way to school I played a tape about Perseus and Medea and my son is still in the dream state induced by imagining Perseus flying about on winged sandals, fighting gorgons backwards while staring into a burnished shield.

Mrs. Stevens, the mother of one of Enrique's classmates, comes huffing by and passes us, muttering at me: "I've NEVER been this late before! Five minutes to the bell!"

"Now, Enrique, your homework is in your lunch box," I say at a propitious moment, when we have moved a few steps closer to the Grade 1 classroom.

"What if my teacher doesn't ask for it?" he says. "She didn't yesterday."

Since the start of school, I have anxiously asked Enrique,

"Any homework today?" And when he replies that he has to cut this or that word beginning with this or that letter from a newspaper, I triumphantly bring out the scissors and make sure he does it. This makes me sleep much better at night. I am actually beginning to feel I am a competent mother.

This morning, however, I hear him muttering: "This is her last chance. If she doesn't call me today, this is the last time I am going to do homework for the whole year." I pretend I haven't heard and place my hand firmly at my son's back and give him an encouraging shove.

Miss Sinclair, the first grade teacher, has glasses and rather messy hair. Purple seems to be her favorite color. Since the start of school, she has worn either a purple blouse or purple skirt or purple high-heeled pumps. Unlike the other teachers, she uses lipstick–a bright mauve shade. I have my doubts about her.

On the first day of school, I confided in her about Enrique's "problem." I waited patiently at the door to the classroom while various well-dressed mothers and fathers trotted their little darlings out for proper introductions. When she finally turned to me, I had it all rehearsed. What I really wanted to say was:

Eight of his classmates have been beating up on Enrique since kindergarten and I won't have it!

Instead, I decided to try another, gentler tack. I said:

It bothers me that Enrique doesn't seem to have any friends. I believe this has affected his self-confidence. I wonder if you could take steps to encourage Enrique to participate more in group activities and games.

I was greatly relieved to see that Miss Sinclair did not seem to take offense at my remarks. She simply nodded impatiently and turned away before I had quite finished.

Rounding the corner to the parking lot, I catch sight of the kindergarten teacher, Mrs. Martin, she of the thick, baby-blue eye shadow and the beak-like nose. I can never forgive her for placing Enrique in the back row during the kindergarten dance program, where I could not see him at all. The big blonde boys like Bryan Thomas, who is surely not a better singer than my Enrique, got to stand in the front row, center, holding the American flag, and he did nothing for the whole hour but fidget and scratch his head. Didn't even open his mouth. While Enrique sang the songs to me endlessly every day–in the bathtub, on the way to school. And during the program, though I couldn't see him at all behind all those blonde bodies, I could hear him singing lustily away (he loved singing the songs—Yankee Doodle Dandy) and I imagined him marching and waving the American flag, as he'd done for me at home.

Enrique has dark hair and very dark skin and very small eyes. He is skinny, too, and is probably the shortest boy in his class.

Thinking back on it, I realize all the children in the back row were non-white. In the back row were Vanessa, the little Hispanic girl; Robby, Nicholas, and Samuel, the three African-American boys; and my Enrique. I remember thinking: Is there some sort of conspiracy going on here? Is Mrs. Martin a subliminal–or perhaps not-so-subtle–racist? But I decide against making my thoughts known, for fear of appearing like another of those strident mommies who constantly find fault with overburdened kindergarten teachers.

The next day, I find myself heading to the library again. I thought I could go cold turkey for a day or two, but the conversation with Miss Sinclair about Enrique might have upset me more than I cared to admit.

At home I find myself standing in wet shoes in the hallway. (It has been raining hard all day, and before going to the library I'd been looking for Christmas tree lights, which involved going from Home Depot to Kmart, in gusty winds). I can't wait and have to crack the book open right then.

I slide out the back way into a bucket of afternoon stars ...

I simply do not understand. I tell myself I have to stop borrowing books like this from the library, books I borrow simply because they have received rave reviews from the *New*

York Times Book Review, which I buy religiously every Sunday. ("Ow, ow, ow" my husband yells suddenly from the guest room, where he has closeted himself all afternoon, watching football. I do not bother to check on him. Earlier, he slipped on a bar of soap in the tub and punched a hole the size of a fist in the side of the shower stall, a feat I had never thought possible ...) What are afternoon stars? What in the world is this narrator trying to say by talking about afternoon stars?

I kneel in front of him, I bow ...

Try, try, try to understand. Understand why this woman is kneeling in front of a character called Will who does the dishes for her church luncheons and whose foot is an open sore, a sore the woman now minutely examines, lifting the bandages tenderly. Try to imagine *myself* kneeling in front of someone who does the dishes and whose foot is an open sore. Try to imagine ...

Her hair looks a little off-center, and that startles me, it is so sad ...

My husband keeps saying unkind things about my mother. She was with us for two weeks in the summer, and during that time he kept suggesting that perhaps I could get her to buy this or that big-ticket item for us. These suggestions strike me as outrageously mercenary, considering that we have already borrowed money from her in the past, and not one cent from his own parents. When I try and suggest that we borrow money from his parents, he immediately cuts me off with, "Out of the question."

She is a 91-year-old woman dying of cancer ...

I am startled by the desire to laugh out loud. But of course, how would the author know? How would anyone know? This is really what it feels like to have someone dying in your family: you will take your mother in your arms, and you will feel her ribs right through the back of her sweater, and you will catch your breath, the fear will rise to your throat, it is a terrible fear that almost blinds you.

This is why I finally decide to put the book down, banish

it to the library, and resolve not to read anymore for a long, long time.

———————

The next day, Enrique excitedly tells me that he has been invited to a birthday party. Of course, it's one of the new boys in school: Thomas Kincaid. His mother seems not to have made any friends at school yet. She is always very nice to me, smiling and nodding whenever we happen to meet at the door to the classroom.

The morning of the party, Enrique sounds strange. He has a cough, but it's a kind I have never heard from him before. In my head I go through a whole arsenal of his past coughs. I try to figure out whether it sounds like a whoop and whether he might have something I have read about in Dr. Spock but never believed (until this moment) actually existed. I consult the Spock (at the same time realizing that many other mothers of six-year-old boys would not be doing this, but what the hell–!)

Under section 750, pertussis:

The character of the cough is cough, cough, cough cough cough cough cough cough–a string of coughs in rapid succession, without a breath in between.

I listen to Enrique and no, he does not go cough, cough, cough cough cough cough cough cough. It is more like one sharp, loud: COUGH! And then a horrible sucking intake of mucus from the nose.

I deliver him to school.

When I pick him up after school, he is listless. Yet I am determined he must not miss this party. I have just spent $20 on a dart blow-gun for Thomas Kincaid. I have wrapped it in my best boys' wrapping paper, the shiny expensive kind decorated with Spitfires and B-52s. I have even forced Enrique to decorate a birthday card saying, "Hi, Tommy!" in his labored, illegible script.   I deliver him to the party, to the waiting arms of smiling, blonde Mrs. Kincaid.

An hour and a half later, I tiptoe into the room where the party boys are gathered. I arrive exactly 10 minutes early, as I had planned. Mrs. Kincaid immediately says:

"He's been coughing a lot."

I am confused by the accusatory tone.

Mrs. Kincaid looks at me. "His cough sounds different. I thought it might just be the bronchitis you told me about last time, but I was listening to him and–"

She pauses a few moments and shakes her head at me. "I'm pretty sure it's the croup."

I stare back at her. What is this "croup"?

"When he sounds like he's barking ..." Mrs. Kincaid endeavors to explain. (Yes! I think. That is exactly how Enrique sounds. Like he's barking ...)

"He sounds like a seal," her husband puts in. He has come up behind me without my noticing. He is a tall, burly man with a silvery gray mustache. He has a gruff voice and I recognize him now as the man who barely glanced at me when I came in. "It's the croup all right."

"It's highly contagious," Mrs. Kincaid is saying. "He should be in bed."

"I'm so sorry," I say. I remember Mrs. Kincaid telling me sometime back that her son Thomas is a very sickly boy. Every winter, he doesn't just catch a cold: he catches pneumonia. She has also told me that when Thomas gets bronchitis, he ends up in the emergency room. I can hardly speak, but I manage to croak out an apology: "I didn't know ..."

I hurry Enrique away.

"Bye, slug!" he calls out cheerfully to the birthday boy (Bark, bark).

In the car, I race home. I can hardly wait to look up this new word in Dr. Spock. Why didn't it occur to me before? Of course! Croup!

The Spock is behind the plant in the living room, where I

put it after I was disgusted with his descriptions of whooping cough. Now I look in the index for the word "cough". There is "whooping cough", and asthma, and asthmatic bronchiolitis, and bronchiolitis, and bronchitis, and "nervous cough" and pneumonia, and sinusitis, and, finally, at the very bottom, "croupy".

How, I ask myself, how could I have missed that word the first time? Perhaps because of the "y" at the end, which confused me? Perhaps because it was at the very bottom of the page?

I put in a call to Enrique's pediatrician. Of course I get his answering service. I tell the lady, "My son has the croup. What I want to know is: is this serious or not? Should I bring him to see a doctor or not?" (Oh tell me, tell me please!)

The woman at the answering service has a flat, nasal voice. She says, "Call the office tomorrow. They'll be open Saturday morning at 8:30. Give them five minutes before you call, all right? Don't call right at 8:30. They need time to get settled."

Obediently, I say, "Thank you," and hang up the phone.

I go back to my son's room. He has crawled into his sleeping bag on the floor and is now fast asleep. I sink down next to him and feel his head. It is bathed in sweat. I listen to his labored breathing. I read the Spock.

But I am restless. After a few moments, I decide it's not enough to wait until the next morning. I call the doctor's answering service again. I tell the lady I want to speak to the doctor. She takes my name and number, and perhaps 15 minutes later the doctor calls. His voice is loud and booms at me over the phone. For the first time, I notice a pronounced drawl. I imagine him on his rounds somewhere, summoning some last ounce of energy or equanimity to deal with this nervous mother, but no matter how hard he tries he is really too tired, and his voice doesn't sound quite natural, therefore the booming.

I grip the phone and write carefully on a piece of paper: cool mist humidifier; Benadryl, 1 1/2 teaspoon; do not wake up; open the window if he has a bad night; continue three or

43

four days; if he doesn't sleep well, Tylenol 1 1/2 teaspoon.

I look at my list after the doctor has hung up. No big deal. No exotic prescriptions. Nothing I couldn't have thought of myself, if I had my wits about me.

Now my son is sleeping quietly. The room is bathed in a cool mist. The weather man on the news says, "Get ready for a cold night."

The old floor heater cranks and heaves manfully.

I call my mother in the Philippines. She, too, has never heard of the croup. She says to pat my son's back with a cupped hand. She says it is good I have the humidifier.

"Give him Vitamin C," my mother says. I remember when we were kids, how she kept huge bottles of Enervon-C in the medicine chest, and we had to take a teaspoon twice a day.

"Give him plenty of liquids," she adds.

It occurs to me that my mother was probably getting ready to go to sleep when I called. I always call when it is late at night there. That's because it is six o'clock in the evening here, and that's the time of day when I am tired and have to find a way to get through cooking dinner.

I can tell from the sound of my mother's voice that she is lying down. Her bed is filled with pillows. They are all clean and smell wonderful. It is a new house, a house I've only visited once before, and it bothers me that views of her in other bedrooms keep intruding.

I imagine her fully stretched out on the bed, totally relaxed. No doubt she was reading something when I called. I want to ask her what. She does not read hungrily, as I do, grabbing books quickly and reading short takes and flinging the books down again when my son calls or when I smell something not quite right in the kitchen. There is a stack of books beside her bed and when she reads she is surrounded by a quiet space of her own making and no one and nothing intrudes on that space. She is very still.

I tell my mother that I have heard things are bad again over there. My mother laughs.

44

"Oh," she says. "It's not that bad. We've lived through the war, we can live through this." (But, I think, it is not war-time. War-time was fifty years ago ...)

I imagine the twelve-hour brownouts, the puddles of water forming beneath the refrigerators, the butter melting, the milk curdling. I imagine Enrique hungry, crying because he does not understand my explanation about why the milk has spoiled. Here he laps it up. It is so good, this American milk.

46

SUTIL

I was last home for my father's funeral. I say "home" even though I am an American citizen now, sworn in with a twenty-piece Navy band in the grand ballroom of the Marriott Hotel on 4th and Mission in San Francisco. Yet, "home" for me was always that other place, that city James Hamilton-Patterson describes as "a parody of the grimmer parts of Milwaukee."

I've never been to Milwaukee, so I can't tell whether this is true or not, whether Manila really is like a parody of a city in the far north of this country (or at least what I imagine to be the far north, in a general region of the country I associate with heavy snow and Laverne and Shirley). But it is different from here, of course. It is the differences I love.

When I was last home, which was for my father's funeral, I slept with my mother in the big wooden four-poster in my parents' bedroom. This bed, handed down from my grandfather, was familiar and reassuring. It was made of heavy wood, a wood that doesn't exist today in any Philippine forest, having been cut to extinction. It may have been called "*molave*." I am not sure of this, as I am not sure of so many things about my culture, which I think I received very young, too young really to understand context or value.

This bed had, instead of a box spring, a woven rattan underside to hold the one thin mattress. And on this mattress, lying next to my mother at night, it seemed to me I could still feel the contours of my father's body, he who lay in the coffin downstairs in the living room, unfamiliar now with the mortician's make-up.

Next to the bed were scattered newspapers, some even from the day my father had his last breakfast, only a few days before. My mother was too distracted to begin putting his things away, and I was glad. It seemed to me that if I stopped thinking for a moment, my father could still be alive. I saw his desk, his bifocals resting on an open page of his appointment book, his pens, the scattered photographs of his grandchildren. His shoes in the closet, his shirts and silk ties, his dressing gown and slippers–all these were still in the room. Even now, as I write this, I see so much of my father, and perhaps because I am not in Manila, where he lived and actually died, it is hard for me to imagine him as really dead, and not just in some foreign city, some city that reminds a British writer of Milwaukee.

It was the cool season in Manila, and therefore we didn't need to run the air conditioner all the time. The windows were wide open. They were barred, screenless windows. From the neighbors' side yard, only a few feet away, I could hear their help coming and going, hear the splash of dirty water being emptied onto the plants, hear the maids chatter as they hung up the laundry, which was clearly visible from my parents' windows.

An attempt had been made to shield us from the view of the neighbors' dirty kitchen. There were a few stunted mango trees, and banana palms. But these were ineffectual.

If I paid attention, I might also smell dogs and chickens– everyone in Manila seemed to keep a menagerie of animals in their backyards, even here in the heart of the city. Everything was dirty and smelled good to me.

In the morning, the maids scrubbed the wooden floors with coconut husks and YCO wax. There was also the smell of frying bacon and fried eggs, fried sausage, fried fish. Everything here seemed bathed in oil, and the oil tasted good, too.

I'd lived for a long time in California. It had been years since I was last home. And I'd forgotten many things about smells and such. But once I was back home, I remembered everything again.

I had two brothers, both still living at home: one was a bachelor and was out all the time. The other was married and had a three-year-old daughter. The daughter and her *yaya* stayed in a room downstairs. My brother and his wife stayed in a room down the hall.

Sometimes, living in California, I forgot that I had brothers. They never wrote, and I heard all their stories second-hand, months after the events in the stories had taken place, usually from one of my mother's letters. Now, back home, it occurred to me that they must also have forgotten they had a sister somewhere in California. Their friends gazed at me with something akin to shock. Perhaps I seemed old to them. I wasn't so much older than my brothers, but in Manila it is still possible to go to discos and other such places well into middle age, and I hadn't done any of those things for a long time.

My brothers didn't say much to me. We would meet each other at breakfast. One or the other would grunt. We would settle down to our meal. They would bury themselves behind the newspapers. Occasionally, someone would gesture to a maid for hot chocolate or *calamansi* juice.

I didn't know whether this reticence was due to the fact that we were still in so much grief from my sister's death in New York, just the year before. My brothers had not been able to fly to New York; they saw the urn of ashes my mother brought back with her–all that was left of my sister. I had cried and my mother had cried, but I hadn't talked to my brothers at all. And so once we were face to face again, we were shy with each other. So much had happened, and it was impossible to talk about anything.

The last time I was home, they had been very young, and so it was hard for me to accept this view of my brothers in coats and ties. I found myself watching them out of the corners of my eyes, as if I might discover a secret, lurking beneath the outlines of their suited shoulders. But I never discovered what it was, really. I ate meekly, head lowered. I couldn't bring myself to gesture to the maids. My hands remained ineffectual, hovering across the table for the butter dish which one of my brothers, with a snap of his fingers, would have summoned a maid for.

We ate breakfast in the same room as my father's coffin. It was a custom that the body could never be left alone, not even for one minute, for the nine days of the wake. But because my father had been such a peaceful man when he was alive, even in death the sight of his coffin did not cause me any heart-rending stirrings of grief. There were tears, yes. But they were quiet tears, and flowed in private. At breakfast, we would just have breakfast. No one talked about the coffin or even referred to it. We knew he would be there for nine days. In a way, he was still with us.

I try to remember if my brother's wife was with us during these breakfasts. My married brother had met his wife at a party at which they were both very drunk. Afterwards, this brother, Ernesto, told my mother that the girl was pregnant. And of course, being the culture that it was, my brother eventually married the girl. Their daughter was born a few months after the wedding. They named her Noelle.

The first week I was back home, I rarely saw my brother's wife. She never came down for breakfast with the rest of us. She was always upstairs in her room, and sometimes I would see one of the maids bringing her up a tray of food. My mother never remarked on this, and so neither did I.

My third night back, I lay in bed sleepless, thinking. There had been a lot of people in the house that morning. The relatives from Bacolod had just arrived–all thirty of them. And we'd had to feed them, of course. Now they were camped out in the living room, on chairs and sofas, determined, like the rest of us, not to leave my father's body alone.

After a long time, I fell asleep. Then, after what seemed only a few minutes, I woke again. There were unfamiliar voices I thought must be coming from the hallway. It took me several minutes to register a man's voice, heavy and slurred. Loud, too. I imagined my bachelor brother drunk, coming home from wherever it was he usually disappeared to at night. Finally it dawned on me that the voices were coming from my married brother and his wife. I don't know how I realized this: the voices seemed a new terrain, an undiscovered country. They were nothing like the mild figures I was used to glimpsing around the house. Perhaps I had a secret knowledge of them that I

50

had been carrying around with me all these past few days, a knowledge that enabled me now to say with certainty: Yes, I recognize those shouts, those moans.

My brother bellowed; my sister-in-law pleaded. The sounds were shattering. My mother threw off the blanket in one quick motion, and from the way she moved, I knew she had done this many times before. That knowledge wounded me. I followed her down the corridor. There it was again: that shattering sound, my sister-in-law pleading, "STOP, STOP, STOP." My brother: "SHUT UP, SHUT UP, SHUT UP!" I saw my mother standing at the door to their room, ear pressed to the heavy wood, listening. I rested my hand on the door knob, saying, "I've had enough of this." My mother's quick pressure on my wrist: I had forgotten how strong her fingers were. The hold she had on me was tight and urgent. "Give them a minute," she said. We stood outside the door, listening. And it was suddenly very silent. So silent I might have thought the earlier sounds were a dream. After a few minutes, my mother and I went back together to the bedroom. Sleepless, we tossed and turned on the big bed, the one where only a few nights earlier my father's body had lain in the depressions of the mattress. For a long time, we didn't speak. We each lay in our cocoons of silence, as far away from each other as we dared. I looked at the water spots on the ceiling. It seemed to me that everything I had just witnessed had changed the whole context of my visit. Finally, I asked my mother: "How long have they been that way?" I thought of my brother as he had been, or as I remembered him from old pictures: he had been chubby and round, his favorite attire when he was five or six a Batman suit. He had a favorite *yaya* named Ning, her complexion dark as a coconut husk, who my brother nevertheless called beautiful and whose breasts he loved to squeeze when he was only four or five. She would slap his hands away, laughing. "*Sutil*" she would say, over and over. "Naughty!"

This was the brother now who was causing his wife to moan and plead: "Stop! No! No!" My hair stood on end. I could not sleep.

The next morning, I saw my brother at the breakfast table. But he looked normal, in control of himself. My sister-in-law must have slipped out somewhere. I looked for my niece. She was in the garden, playing with her *yaya*.

"Noelle! Noelle, come here!" I called, insistent.

"Whadisit?" she lisped, walking to me with her little bow and arrow.

I held her close. She smelled of sweat and Johnson's baby powder. I looked at her face, lifted her chin with my hand. I tried to see something of my brother in the little girl. There was something, very slight: the black, curly hair; perhaps the pudgy cheeks. But I couldn't be sure. And I wanted to be sure.

My mother had told me that my brother hadn't been the first. This was something. And he and the girl had relations only that one night, the night they met. Afterwards, when she became pregnant, we told my brother, "Get a blood test." But he refused. And now this.

The day continued, and everyone went about on their own business: my mother went out with friends; my bachelor brother and the married brother went to work. I asked the maids: did you hear anything last night? And they told me they were used to seeing glasses lying broken on the floor, or cracked mirrors.

That night there was a family gathering in my aunt's house. A cousin volunteered to stay with my father's body; the rest of us went to my aunt's. She lived in a suburb just outside Manila. We had to drive down the South Super Highway, which was crowded with commuter traffic and buses and jeepneys. There was a confusing intersection with an overpass, where there seemed to be a lot of pedicab stands and vendors' stalls, where the aroma of barbecued pork was very strong and mingled with the garbage smells from the street. It was also poorly lit, and in the shadows I saw figures darting in and out of the traffic, some with long poles balanced on their shoulders, others brandishing cartons of cigarettes at passing cars. After making a right turn here, we were suddenly in wide, well-paved streets lined with large houses and tall gates.

We were having dinner, and my brother and his wife walked in. They were hand-in-hand. He nuzzled her hair and cheek. She laughed. I looked at them and lost all my appetite. I thought of the little girl, Noelle, sleeping peacefully at home. This morning Noelle had bit her *yaya* on the belly. Why did she do that? Bad girl! we all scolded. The *yaya* had cried. There was blood. Her name was Imelda; she was a very young girl, from the provinces. Looking at her, anyone could tell she was not happy.

Later this Imelda came to me and asked for some money. I gave her some. Later I asked my brother: "Has she asked you for some money lately?" And he said no.

I remained two more weeks in my parents' house, with my brother and his wife just down the corridor, and for the rest of my time there, I didn't sleep well, although there were no more disturbing sounds from the other room.

After the traditional nine-day wake, during which time we were successful in never leaving my father's body alone, even for a minute, and during which time our family entertained hordes of guests who came from as far away as Iloilo, we cremated my father's body and placed the ashes in an urn in the family crypt.

During all this time, my mother and I were unable to shed a tear. I kept busy making a list of all the people who had sent us mass cards. This task kept me occupied for hours at a time. We stacked the mass cards on the dining room table, and there were six piles, each a couple of feet high. My mother ordered engraved cards, so that we could reply to everyone.

My sister-in-law continued to flit in and out, but she was not part of the funeral arrangements. One day I was surprised when she joined us at breakfast. I found myself becoming unexpectedly talkative, talking about all sorts of people I really didn't know very well.

My sister-in-law came from a rich family. Yau. Chinese *mestizo*. She was very fair, much fairer than my brother, and she had porcelain skin and light brown hair that made her look almost Spanish. Her eyes, too, were pale and rather watery, as though filmed over constantly with tears. She had a wan way of moving, but I heard people say she loved to go dancing and was quite a good dancer. On nights when my brother was out of town, she went with a group of friends to the disco. She had married my brother when she was only 19, and already four months pregnant with Noelle. It was a mistake, the pregnancy. She'd only just met my brother. But people said they were both very drunk. So that was the reason for the tension in the family. And I cringed thinking of my father, who was always so decorous and correct, lying awake at night, listening to glasses shattering against walls, listening to the low moaning sounds my sister-in-law made at night. My mother told me it happened all the time. But they were always so sweet and loving the next morning–no one could understand it, and so my parents just left them alone. But my brother's voice is slurred and thick, and though rather slow-witted, or because he is slow-witted, his anger is a scary thing which he knows very well how to use, striking with it (though I cannot imagine he has actually used physical violence, this thought is so repugnant to me I immediately shut it out of my mind) here and there and reducing my sister-in-law to that voice, that voice moaning "Stop! Stop!"

After three weeks, I returned to my house in California. It seemed I didn't sleep very well there, either. Nights I would lie awake in bed, thinking. Or, in the kitchen, when I had my hand on the refrigerator door, to open it, to pull out an opened can of evaporated milk for my coffee; a piece of Wonder Bread for my breakfast, I would be struck by something: a color, a wash of white, the way the bread looked in its bright red, white and blue plastic wrapping. I could imagine someone painting the primary colors, the wash of white that hurt my eyes. And then I would think of THEM, my brother and my sister-in-law, in that other place, that place of heat and complex smells, and I would stop in mid-gesture, not knowing whether I meant to tuck a strand of hair behind my ear, or to continue getting the milk or bread.

Suddenly, the present would be overtaken by a vision of hot rooms, tangled sheets, and cracked mirrors. I saw bedclothes trailing to the floor, which was littered with shards of glass. The room would be empty. I would stand at the doorway, looking around for my brother and my sister-in-law, who I somehow knew were not there. I would see my reflection in the cracked mirror. In my mind I heard again the words of the *yaya*, gone so many years, saying over and over, "*Sutil!*"

SELENA

Selena was leaning over her desk. Vic had known her for—what?—six years. He hadn't yet been able to tell her about the e-mail he'd found: the one from the engineer in Purchasing, who'd said he wanted to fuck her. He'd found the crumpled-up piece of paper in his "in" box. When he'd picked it up, annoyed, something had made him open it, read what it contained. He'd blanched at the words, addressed to "Dearest Selena": *When I'm in the office, I really want to fuck you!! Your lips, your voice, your touch. Oh, how can you control yourself? I can't anymore …*

The company he worked for, Quadrus, was an up-and-coming starter in the East Bay. The low glass building lay in a cul-de-sac, surrounded by other companies with names like Trend, Cygnus, Silica. Most days, he dealt with reliability problems and wrote Quality Systems Assessments for the Chairman on the corrective actions he had implemented. The emphasis in Quadrus was on maintaining high yields; reliability was only a consideration if a customer complained. He'd been a manager for three years and in that time had experienced a slow erosion of confidence. He was caught in the middle—wanting to do a good job, yet hurrying, always hurrying to approve a product before it went out the door. He had twelve product lines to look out for; there was always a defect in one batch or another. The gray in his hair had multiplied, and deep furrows had been carved on his forehead, the sides of his cheeks. He clenched his teeth at night.

Selena was Vic's primary assistant. She reported directly to him, and had done so for almost three years. She had white, white skin—perhaps almost as white as his wife's. Today she was wearing a black camisole and, over that, a crocheted thing with large holes—a peek-a-boo look. One shoulder of the crocheted top was tugged down, revealing bare skin. Her chest rose and fell, rose and fell.

She looked up, caught him staring. He turned quickly and headed for the door, but not before he thought he had seen a small smile begin to form at the corners of her mouth. That mouth was sometimes a shiny red, or pink, depending on what lipstick she had applied that morning, and outlined carefully with a lip pencil, the cupid's bow just so. She had teeth of blinding whiteness, straightness—*she must have had the work done here, after she got out of Viet Nam.* Only in America could she have acquired such teeth.

He was ashamed of his own, botched by a Philippine orthodontist, the cheapest because his father didn't believe in throwing away money on such trifles.

The inner rims of Selena's eyes were always lined with black. They made her look mysterious.

And the whiteness of her skin! Perhaps she powdered it, yes—skin of such an impossible whiteness.

Her two little boys—sometimes she brought them in with her, to show them off. She had given them American names: Ian and Timmy. Her Vietnamese husband lurked nearby, bowing his head in embarrassment. The boys had their mother's fair complexion. But Vic privately thought them ugly. Like their father. He with the thick glasses, who seemed far too old for Selena. *Perhaps it was an arranged marriage.*

————————

"What'chu want?" Selena said to him plaintively. Her voice was throaty and deep, and she threw it out without hesitation. She had a way of popping into his office at odd moments. "Hey!" she would call out, in a way that was at once aggressive and familiar. Even if he happened to be on the phone with his wife, he would hang up quickly, flustered. "I've gotta go!" he would say hoarsely into the phone, to his wife's confusion. "Why?" she would ask. "There's a vendor on the other line!" he would croak, barely managing to get the lie out. Selena would be standing there, unconcernedly prattling away. She knew she had him. *She knew.* When had all this started? Now he couldn't help a flush creeping over his cheeks, whenever she caught him staring. He had to drop his eyes. He was her manager, it wasn't seemly, but—

Maybe he have problems at home, Selena thought to herself.

58

She was supremely bored in the office. Her last flirtation, with the engineer in Purchasing, had ended rather abruptly when Jerry Sato, his manager, had happened upon one of their e-mails. Jerry had not looked kindly on their use of company time to exchange what amounted to almost daily missives, concerned with touching and uncontrollable emotion. He had taken the matter to Personnel. So, that was ended. That was over.

For years she had known Vic had a soft spot for her. He could never deny her anything when she wrapped her arms around his shoulders and pleaded. *Come on,* she would say. *Let us off early, just this once.* He would nod, never looking her directly in the eye.

Vic was Filipino. What did that mean, anyway? The Filipinos she had known were mostly men. Filipino men knew how to talk, but Vic didn't. The last Filipino engineer who had been with the company had seduced her and for a few months they had had a tempestuous affair. But he had gone back to his wife and left the company. It was around that time that Vic joined the department. Perhaps because she had been hurt over the other engineer, she barely noticed him.

Vic was quiet, and he was a little shy. *Private,* she called him, teasing. His skin was lighter than the others', and his nose was straight and pointed, giving him almost a Latino look. His best friend was Dan, an engineer in Reliability. The two were always together. Dan had recently broken up with his wife. Now he and Vic were always going together for drinks after work, to Chevy's or to Elephant Bar.

Selena's uniqueness lay in her voice. She had a strong accent but she wasn't ashamed to speak aggressively. *These Americans, that's all they understand,* she thought. It was the stance, the aggression, that brought you respect. She knew it didn't hurt that she was pretty. Men melted before her pretty face, with that aggressive mouth. They called her "honey", "sweetheart." She smiled, she laughed, she loved the attention. Her last boss, Roy, had looked longingly at her one day and said, "I have misplaced myself."

Now Vic was talking to her about Lots Inspected, Lots Rejected, and the Lot Rejection Rate. He leaned over, quite close. She noticed that lately he didn't like to speak to her husband, when her husband dropped by. He almost never commented on the pictures of her two sons that she had taped to the walls of her cubicle. One day, she surreptitiously took them down. She noticed that Vic seemed more at ease.

Selena remembered when she became visibly pregnant with her second child. She moved slowly through the office corridors, feeling lazy and tired, as if she were pushing away the air. But the roundness of her belly seemed to attract Vic. Once or twice, he'd ask to rest his hand on it. They'd gone out to lunch at a Chinese restaurant. Often, she would refuse him, but that day she'd said yes. It was a beautiful day, a week before Christmas. She felt reckless, disjointed. He'd asked to put a hand on her belly and she'd said, *all right,* laughing. The look on his face: he seemed reverent, close to tears. She hadn't known, until that moment, that a pregnant woman could be sexy. Now she felt it, her power.

When the child came, she was away from the office for a month. When she returned, her first day back, she was able to slip into her old jeans. When she'd bumped into Vic, later that morning, his eyes had registered surprise and pleasure. The pleasure in his eyes made her feel silky and beautiful. She stretched her arms languidly above her head in his presence, letting her blouse tighten over her breasts, full with breast milk. She twisted her hair up into a French knot, laughing as she did so. Blinding him with her beauty, the whiteness of her arms.

After that, she always took care to stand close to him. She could feel his breath quicken—little, shallow breaths. And then one day, she smelled it, the difference: he had worn cologne. She said nothing, only smiled to herself.

His wife was a teacher, this she knew. At one time, he used to talk about her. Now, when she inquired, he would grimace and shrug, as if the subject were somehow a painful one. She stood closer and closer, and once even leaned her thigh against his one day, when he was showing her a report he wanted her to correct. He said nothing, but he hadn't moved away, either. After that, when she was sure no one was looking, she would rest a hand on his arm, or adjust his tie. She would playfully pull a strand of his black hair. She, too, began to wear cologne—a strong scent, animal and musky, that seemed to please him. She made sure she entered his office as often as possible, to leave her scent there after she'd left the room.

———————

Vic liked to picture her growing up in Viet Nam with her family. He imagined her at its center, a warm, ripe peach. Her name then had been Thuy. He thought: *her parents must have loved her very much*. They would have protected her fiercely, during the fall of Saigon and its aftermath. And afterwards, when they'd moved to the Bay Area from the refugee camp in Hong Kong, when she was 16. They must have watched over her.

She'd wanted to be as American as possible. They even let her change her name. Thuy became Selena, after that Tejana singer, the one who was tragically killed by her manager, the one whose life had been made into a movie starring Jennifer Lopez. Perhaps there was bad luck in the name but Thuy cared only that it had belonged to a singer with flashing dark eyes, a seductive smile.

Her parents sent her to college. To San Jose State. Only she hadn't been able to finish her program. She had dropped out. *Why?* She hadn't told him. She'd dropped out in her sophomore year. *Was she pregnant?* But he knew that she had only the two children, and both with John. Now she wanted to go back to school. She had asked him to negotiate on her behalf with the company, to get them to pay her tuition. He would do it! She was very deserving. There was no one more deserving in the whole company.

———————

At home she was always tired. Her husband, John, was ineffectual with their two toddlers. He was a much older man; what did she expect? He was almost 50. She yelled at him: "You stupid!" she would say. "You don't know how to change diaper?" He would bow his head meekly. She hadn't allowed him near her since the second baby was born.

Vic's home was always a mess. His wife came home drained from her job teaching Composition and Rhetoric at a local community college. "The kids are so developmentally behind!" she would rant. She would stretch out on the couch, a discouraged look on her face. Her classes had over thirty students. She taught three of them each quarter.

He had little to offer her by way of comfort. They needed her job. He could not countenance her quitting to stay home and write full time, which he knew was what she really wanted to do. *Maybe later,* he thought. *After our son is through with high school and college.*

Sometime in the afternoon, she suggested they take a walk. The dog hadn't been walked in over a week. He agreed. As usual, their son, Johnmel, refused to go along. It was just him and Malou then, walking the chilly, quiet streets.

Without knowing exactly why, he found himself confessing, "You know, I can't seem to get it up anymore." Malou looked at him quizzically. Sex did not concern her. He'd never been any good at it, and after a while it seemed to him that she'd preferred not to have to put up with his fumbling exertions. It was amazing to him, still, that they'd had the one child. That had been almost fourteen years ago.

"How do you know?" Malou asked.

Trapped. He should have thought before speaking. But he had an easy familiarity with her; she had been so comfortable with him, for so many years.

"I just know," he said, hastily.

"It bothers you," she said. It was a statement. There was a tinge of wonder in her voice. Had she never really thought about the subject? What did she do all day, when she was in her department at the college? Was she never approached by a male colleague or a student–? This line of thinking made him nervous. He began to feel a trickle of sweat down the back of his neck.

"No," he said. "It doesn't."

She didn't say anything more. They continued walking the dog in silence.

There were four women in Vic's department at Quadrus. In the beginning, their constant squabbling made it difficult for him to concentrate. Each of them wanted his full attention: there was Nellie, the pretty Lebanese-American. Thin, dark, and quick, she loved to engage the male engineers in easy, bantering talk that hovered on the verge of risqué. There was Julie, a quiet Indian-American who nevertheless conducted a not-so-secret affair with a young engineer in Wafer Fabrication; Helen, the chesty document-control technician with the loud mouth; and Selena.

Helen and Selena were always fighting. He noticed they fought more after Selena had her second boy. He thought it might be because Helen was jealous. Helen had told him one day that she couldn't have children. And Helen was busty but she was not pretty. She did work hard, though. Sometimes, after he had spent some time with Selena in her cubicle, laughing and joking, he would feel bad at the sight of Helen, alone at her desk, pretending to read messages off her computer. He would then go over to Helen and allow her to tug at his hair, to play with his tie. Once, Leo, the Filipino technician, had taken a Polaroid of him with Helen, during one such playful moment. It made everyone in the department tease them. He was glad. He didn't mind anyone thinking it was Helen he flirted with, because it would not be true.

Eventually he'd hit on the practice of bringing in little presents for the "girls" now and then: boxes of Godiva chocolates; candy his mother-in-law brought from the Philippines. But they were really presents for Selena. She liked chocolates, she happened to mention one day. After that, when he was in a store with his wife, he'd bought a box of truffles. His wife, if she had noticed the purchase at all, had chosen to say nothing.

The next day, when he'd brought the chocolates to the office, there were "oooohs" and "aaahs" from all the girls. But it was Selena he watched. Oh, what joy when he saw her take one and pop it whole into her tiny mouth. She ran a small, moist tongue over her lips afterwards, and laughed when she saw him looking.

———————

Selena lived in a small blue house off a major thoroughfare. He'd driven by there once, out of curiosity. It was a Saturday. He'd expected Malou to take Johnmel to a friend's house. Usually she stayed and chatted with the other mother for an hour or so. He backed his car out of the driveway and headed across the bridge, to a neighborhood of tract houses near the office, a neighborhood he knew as Little Viet Nam.

The street was narrow. He had to drive slowly. On either side were large old cars, some rusted and dented. The large boat in front of her house had a FOR SALE sign on the rear-window.

The house was shuttered and still. A rickety wooden fence enclosed the back yard. Peering through the slats, he'd seen a small yard, overgrown with weeds. A neighbor was out on the driveway, washing his car, and glanced up curiously as he drove by. He was embarrassed, thinking that the neighbor might remember his car, and mention it to her. Yet the neighbor might have thought he, too, was Vietnamese. Filipinos and Vietnamese didn't look all that different from one another, after all.

Afterwards, driving home, he'd mused about her. He'd wondered if she and her husband had gone away for the weekend—why were the shutters drawn? And what could be the meaning of the large sign on the front lawn: THIS HOUSE IS PROTECTED BY SECURITY? And the stickers advertising same on the windows? Who could possibly want to break into that house?

He'd remembered her complaining to him that she'd been receiving some mysterious phone calls at work. He'd obliged her by putting a trace on her line. The calls, it turned out, came from all over: Palo Alto, Pleasanton. One even came all the way from Santa Barbara. She had no idea who might be calling her. Her face, as she told him, assumed a look of grave anxiety. Her large eyes crinkled up and seemed about to overflow with tears. He might have put his arm around her at that moment, if that fat slug Lew had not been just around the corner, in the next cubicle, listening.

"Where have you been?" Malou said. "I've been trying to call you all afternoon."

"I had to see a vendor," he said.

"On a *Saturday?*" Malou said. Her face had stitched itself into a tight knot.

"Why? What's wrong? Can't I go somewhere for a few hours without you throwing a fit anymore?"

Before she could answer, he'd walked away.

Going down the hallway, he peeked into his son's bedroom. There he was, playing on his computer again. He was a gnome in a role-playing computer game called Everquest. Sometimes, Vic glanced at the screen when his son was playing, and saw fat hairy bugs (most of these ended up flat on their backs, scaly legs waving at the sky), skeletons waving swords, troll-like creatures. He would hear his son giggle and laugh, his orthodontia ($2,500 worth) gleaming in the light from the desk lamp.

Johnmel had nightmares; he cried out in his sleep. Sometimes, when Vic passed his bedroom door, he could hear the sound of Johnmel's raspy breath, and the grinding of his teeth. One day he'd come home with bruises necklacing his arms. "Who did this? Who did this?" Malou had shouted, over and over, the tendons standing out from her neck. Johnmel had refused to answer, hanging his head and wiping away angry tears.

Of course, there were whispers. Inevitably. Complaints that his department's productivity was declining. Layoffs. Eventually, he was called into the Chairman's office.

"Are you and Selena having an affair?" the Chairman asked.

Vic didn't answer.

"If you don't answer me now, you're out of a job," the Chairman had said.

Vic had felt it, the hole opening up at the pit of his stomach. He was suddenly furious. To be talked at in that way. As if he were a child. He was a manager! He was in charge of a department.

65

He had 19 years of experience in Quality Control. Daily he walked the floor, inspecting batches of product. The chemicals in the air sometimes made him dizzy. He had headaches all the time, from the fumes. The stains on his fingernails from handling chemicals would never go away.

He'd denied it. He'd denied everything. But it hadn't saved his job. He'd been laid off the following month.

He did know this: the leaving of Quadrus filled him with a terrible sadness. Sometimes he equated this sadness with the loss of Selena's presence in the mornings. He imagined her going to work, flinging her bag on the chair (she was always running in late), and clicking on her computer with anxious fingers. He saw her frown, her expression of concentration. He knew who her new manager was; they had talked often on the phone. Sometimes this new manager, Ken, would say: "Selena's here. Would you like to say 'hi'?" And he always said yes. He would hear Ken murmuring in the background. Then Selena would take the phone with a laugh. Her voice, her rich, loud voice, always filled him with a tremendous ache.

On weekends he imagined her sitting on the living room floor with her boys, playing. Her eyes were alive with love and maternal pride. She would throw them little balls and call out, "Catch! Catch!" Her husband was never there; he had become shadowy, a mere presence. He was not an entity; he did not count.

And there were many many days when he longed to be looking over her work again. He remembered the previous spring, when they had worked together on the Quality Policy Manual. How they had had to work late, and often gotten take-out from the Chinese restaurant across the street. Her hands sorting through the pages of the report were quick and long-fingered. Sometimes he had had the overwhelming urge to take them in his own. But he had restrained himself.

One day he actually found himself dialing her home number. "Hello!" she said, her voice bright and forceful. He'd taken in his breath, sharply. "Hel-loooo!" she'd said again, impatient. He'd put down the phone.

Now he would invite this or that Quadrus manager out to lunch, ostensibly to indulge in a little "boy talk." Really it was for the purpose of finding out how Selena was doing. Ken told him that Selena was looking for another job. Vic worried about this. In another company, would there be people who would try to take advantage of her, as the other Quadrus engineer had done? Would they recognize her gift, her tremendous talent for numbers, and reward her appropriately? He knew that if she ever left Quadrus, she would call to ask him for a reference. He looked forward to being of service to her once again.

In the meantime, he almost never dressed up anymore to go out. He wore old jeans around the house, frayed at the hems. He wore old T-shirts. Malou never complained. She did his laundry and ironed his shirts with a stoic air. One day she said, "I feel old. You make me feel old." He didn't know what to say in response, so he'd kept silent.

An old classmate of his from the Philippines, who was now a big-shot, the President of his own consulting company in the Valley, called to offer him a job. He'd accepted, but found it intolerable and left after only two months. There were anxious phone calls between Malou and his classmate.

"What's wrong with him?" the old classmate had asked Malou.

"I don't know. A mid-life crisis, maybe?" Then Malou had told him about Selena.

"It's not deep," the classmate had said. "Whatever they had, I know it's not deep."

Vic had overheard them on the phone one day. He'd wanted to laugh. Who knew what was really going through his mind, in those days? No one—and certainly not Malou.

Malou had sighed. The role of a victimized wife was beginning to grow on her.

What was it about working for another Filipino that had irked him so? His friend drove a Mercedes convertible. He was divorced, shared custody of his one child, and had a girlfriend fifteen years his junior. He had hired Vic to be his Vice President in charge of

Quality Control. But after a few weeks, it seemed he didn't want Vic talking to the customers anymore. He told Vic to go through Mike, who was American and much younger. Vic was humiliated. He felt it showed his classmate's lack of trust. They'd had a sharp exchange of words; everyone in the office heard.

That night, he'd gone home and told Malou he was quitting. Her face immediately took on a look of panic. He'd typed out a letter of resignation right there on the dining room table. The next few weeks, he stayed home, letting his beard and nails grow and drinking beers on the living room couch.

And one day he decided to drive over to Selena's house. Just to say hello, he told himself. He parked on a side street and waited. He noted that she'd planted roses along the perimeter fence. And, getting down from his car and peeking through a gap in the side fence, he'd seen gardening tools scattered haphazardly on the grass. "She must be happy," he told himself, and thus felt himself become less miserable.

He waited a long time, for what seemed like hours but was perhaps only a matter of minutes. He saw the neighbors driving by. No one so much as glanced at him. But she herself never appeared.

He began to grow anxious, knowing Malou would be looking for him. When he wasn't home, she looked through his things. It was something she'd taken to doing, in the last six months. She tried to be discreet, but he could always tell when his papers had been moved. And so he'd had to carefully hide the Polaroids of Selena that he'd carefully hoarded over the years. He'd had to put them in a box in the garage, up high on a shelf where he knew Malou would never think to look.

———————

Finally, one day, he saw her. It was completely unexpected—he was eating by himself at a Japanese restaurant close to his new company, a medical equipment manufacturer called ProVantage. And there she was.

She came in with a large group—perhaps six or seven people, mostly people from Quadrus. Boisterous and loud, they'd taken a table towards the back. Walking across the room, no one looked in his direction. He was able to pick out familiar faces: Mike, the engineer from Manufacturing; John Burns, the vice president of Purchasing. And why was she with these people? He noticed John place a proprietary hand on the small of Selena's back as he pulled out a chair for her. Selena tossed her head back and laughed. She'd placed a slender hand on John's arm. She was wearing a red coat (it was chilly), one he recognized. Her long hair was tied back in a style she'd worn only for office parties or other special occasions.

He decided to walk over as soon as he had finished his lunch.

"Hi," he'd said, and the whole group turned to look at him.

There were hearty greetings, hands extended. Selena had smiled. (She was prettier when she smiled.) He'd bent down to plant a kiss on her cheek. He'd smelled her perfume. The men joked and laughed. Everyone was happy. He'd even pulled up a chair. He'd sat beside Selena, and she'd laughed. Now and then, leaning forward, his knee brushed her thigh. He noticed she didn't attempt to move away. His soul leapt. He thought: I am happy now.

But, before he knew it, they were saying they had to go. He gave them all his office number. He told them he had a great job, and he was happy. Selena said, "I'm so glad." She said, "Drop by and see us sometime." He promised he would.

When he was seated behind the wheel of his car, he put his head down on the steering wheel and wept. Then, after a few moments, he straightened up and wiped his face. He chewed a breath mint. He tried to breathe deeply.

Cars had collected around him. The air was breezy. The sky was, he noticed suddenly, a startling blue. Love, he thought, was painful, but also something grand. He drove back to his office, his heart light.

EXTINCTION

My name is Warren Dupré Smith. I am what is known as an arboreal expert. A few years ago, I was assigned to do fieldwork in the islands of P_____, which stretch 1,850 kilometers directly across the equator in a north-south configuration. I knew nothing about these islands other than that they are the world's second-largest archipelago after Indonesia. The land area is roughly 300,439 kilometers, or approximately the size of Italy, but its fragmented layout gives it a long total coastline of about 18,000 kilometers.

I had gone to P_____ under the auspices of a United Nations grant to teach the people about trees. In those islands, this particular form of plant life had almost grown extinct. The few trees that existed, in isolated pockets in the interior, were very small. I counted a total of 132 trees in the entire archipelago, and the largest of these was not more than 6 centimeters in diameter and about 10 meters high. In my box of letters I have a detailed arboreal report with photographs of plant specimens and descriptions that include family, genus, species, and plant age.

The coastlines were bare, and the soil on which the people had built their homes was slowly washing out to sea. Thus there was great fear and trepidation in the coastline villages, and the people there generally exhibited the clinical symptoms of depression.

I made my home in a valley roughly 8 kilometers long and 5 kilometers wide, in the province of S_____. Oval in shape, this valley was surrounded by a low rim of hills with fairly steep escarpments. Interspersed among the ravines grew loose thickets of bamboo. One side of the valley opened out to a narrow beach. In the mornings I walked down to the sand and observed the almost imperceptible movement of the waves. I imagined that in a decade or two, there would not be anything left of the beach, or of the escarpments surrounding it. Occasionally, as I poked my toes in the sand, I saw bits of glass (the people in those islands were very fond of trinkets) and cigarette butts (they were also fond of American cigarettes, which they universally referred to as "Blue Seal").

My days in P_____ were long and filled with galling disappointments. The people were small and dark and thin, and a strange odor arose from their bodies in the late evenings, as though they had been swimming in oil and had just now come up for a bath.

They knew about shade but they had forgotten about the particular shadows made by leaves and branches. I felt it was important to expand their knowledge in this direction. They were disbelieving when I told them about tree roots, how they snake across the soil, looking for water. Perhaps they confused my descriptions of roots with some malignant form of animal life. Their eyes, still and dark, like pools, gazed out at me, expressionless.

A long time ago, the people of P_____ had put their history down on the bark of trees. They had used leaves as books, and reeds as pens to scratch their flowing script. Since the trees have expired, these people have lost their history.

I thought I felt nothing for the place but later, when I was back home, I missed certain things: the dry soil; the blank, expressionless faces of the people. And I made a list. A list of remembered things. I put the list away in a safe place.

A year ago, I began to look for the list again. In a moment of reflection—perhaps it was the angle of light from my window, one late summer afternoon, bringing to mind a beach, a hut, a path– I thought about the time I had spent away from home. Years, it had been.

But the box where I thought I had kept the list safe was empty. A teakwood box, of the dark wood the people of P_____ called *molave*. A tree that, generations ago, was known to grow in brackish swamps, whose wood was said to be impervious to fire. I hunted in desk drawers, in closets, in all the shelves in the house. But the list was gone.

And then I began to try and remember what I had written. The shreds of memory came slowly. You know how one pulls a skein of scarves apart, after they have been left tangled in a heap in a corner. That was what remembering was like for me. It was a process that lasted many months. This is how I came to write the following pages:

THE FRAMEWORK

Studies have shown that the earth is a dynamically evolving body. My sketches of the volcanic and tectonic cycle in P_____ naturally show the interaction of sedimentation, volcanic activity, precipitation and evaporation on a particular stretch of coastline, running the length of the province of S_____. Natural disasters had long been a fact of life in this region, the number of deaths resulting from high-velocity winds being 627,211 in the twenty-year span that I lived in the islands; and earthquakes and volcanic eruptions 579,689. There were, in addition, a very small number of deaths – 27,065 deaths – attributable to floods.

THE LAND

The soil of P_____ was a heavy, dark red color. An analysis of this soil, conducted by Professor B_____ , revealed it to be rich in metals, particularly aluminum, copper, and iron. Curiously, the people seemed to have no ability to transform these metals into implements, for the tools they used were of the simplest stone.

There were large patches of residual limestone in the hills. The limestone rock was compact and, on fracture, creamy white. I sometimes found mollusc shells imbedded in these rocks, even at the highest elevations. The shells were colored an iridescent blue.

The soil of the lowlands was loose and sedimentary. Riverbanks had superficial deposits of sand. Mudflows were not uncommon.

BOTANICAL PROPERTIES

P_____ was a tropical country, once renowned around the world for its forests of exotic hard wood: *narra, molave, kamagong.*

All species of trees that are now extinct.

The *narra* tree reached a height of 25 meters or more. Its leaves were 15 to 30 centimeters long. Its panicles were axillary and branched, its flowers numerous and yellow. It flowered in April and May.

The *molave* tree reached a height of 15 meters. Leaflets were shining, glabrous. Flowers, blue. Found in dry thickets, the wood was so hard that any house built with *molave* was said to be fairly indestructible, even by fire.

I could not find any descriptions of the *kamagong* tree, but was fortunate to meet a family that had several dark bowls made of this wood in their possession. The bowls had apparently been handed down for many generations. The family used the bowls for decorative purposes only, and the reason for this became apparent to anyone who held a bowl in one's hands: the feeling aroused by this common object was remarkably akin to prayer.

FLORA AND OTHER FORMS OF NATIVE LIFE

Being so close to the Equator, the daily temperature was uniformly over 100 degrees Fahrenheit. And there were many flowers. And these flowers grew in such profusion and magnificence that people were often confused and mistook them for animals.

Yes, these animated flowers seemed to have their own inner vitality, an inner vitality of motion.

Perhaps the people who lived in that place walked around in the middle of a hallucination.

In this hallucinatory country there were also all species of vines and creeping plants. These species had been described and documented over a hundred years ago by the learned Augustinian

74

friar Domingo Blanco, who in his "Flora de F_____" (1st edition, 1837) had named almost 15,000 varieties. If you go to the great library of Seville, even today, and ask to speak to the Director, Jose Valladolid, he will show you the large heavy books with the brittle paper, the originals of the books Father Blanco had published in the early 19th century.

In addition to this bewildering array of plants, there was fungi in all the colors of the rainbow, sprouting after only a few hours on food left standing on the kitchen counters. There was an abundance of mold, worms, and vermin.

The vermin were large and black, with short scuttling legs and long black feelers. They crawled out of the walls and out of the drain pipes and one had to be careful where one stepped at all times. If one happened to put his or her foot next to one of these pests, they would bite. A few hours later the two tiny red puncture marks would flare up into white boils: two of them, side by side, barely grazing, like two planets held in a stable orbit, or two stars in a binary system, like Alpha Centauri. A few days later these boils would erupt with a strange yellow ooze. Then a fever would come, and sometimes that person survived but more often that person succumbed and expired. This fever was called "the fever of the vermin." The people lit candles to ward off such bad luck from befalling them.

Large brown worms crawled through the ground, under the garbage which people left lying on the streets. (The people had very poor notions of sanitation.) Because of the worms, the garbage was in motion at all times. From afar, the streets looked like heaving brown seas. The pungent odor of rotting detritus penetrated all corners of the houses.

The people were also blessed reproductively. Each family had 14 children, at least. These active little creatures swarmed over the city streets, arms outstretched for coins.

SEASONS

There was a hot season and a cool season. During the

hot season, the wind known as *Amian* blew from the north; during the cool season, a wind known as *Dugudug* blew from the east, across the sea from China. When the people knew the *Dugudug* was coming, their voices assumed an added lilt. Sometimes, from the sound of so many voices saying the word together, the heavens opened up and torrential rain poured down, obliterating the streets.

During the season of the *Dugudug*, the people were happy. They went around unclothed.

HISTORY

The earliest people to settle in P_____ were a Negroid people of uncommonly short stature, most of whom can still be found living in the most remote mountain areas. A species of legume were the staple diet of these people. They were thought to be most prevalent on the mountain ranges of nearby Bolotan, a few miles from my valley. Travelling through Bolotan, I perceived a lunar landscape where once trees and foliage painted the surrounding areas a shade of green. I did not then see one of these strange people, though I looked carefully in the shadows among the mountain crevices

I was told by my guide that there had been no actual sightings for many generations, but a few years ago there was the curious case of Nestor. He appeared quite unexpectedly one morning, rooting for food in a pigsty behind a farmer's hut. The general consensus was that the vegetation on Bolotan must have been drastically reduced, and therefore the man was apparently starving. Unfortunately, the farmer, never having seen a Negrito before, was frightened out of his wits. He grabbed a large knife and slew the poor creature. Then the farmer's intent had been to eat him, but he was fortunately prevented from doing so by the local authorities. The corpse was transported to the capital city of T_____, there to be dissected by Dr. Z, the most renowned doctor in the land. During his examination of the body, Dr. Z made a remarkable discovery: he claimed to have found that the man had two hearts, nestled one on top of the other, in the chest cavity.

In the book Dr. Z. later wrote about his discovery, he theorized that the two hearts beat in a strange rhythm, one-two-three, one-two-three, one-two-three, instead of our normal ka-thump ka-thump. In the words of Dr. Z, "It was as if these two hearts had been dancing a waltz together." The man with two hearts was thereafter known as Nestor, after the country's foremost dancer.

There was a great push to hunt down another specimen and expeditions were sent to the mountains of Bolotan to search for additional Negritos. But these small people are extremely shy and are furthermore quite wily. They have thus far managed to avoid capture, perhaps by hiding in caves.

In my discussions with Dr. Z, he disclosed that the teeth of the said Negrito had a strange configuration. They pointed backwards, like those of the great white sharks I had sometimes seen in natural history museums. The jaw, too, was unusually prominent.

Dr. Z had taken it upon himself to have the specimen stuffed. It now stands in a corner of his study, and whenever I visited, I could not shake the feeling that the creature was staring at me dully, with its opaque eyes. No doubt it stands there still, if Dr. Z himself is still alive, still teaching, in the University I remember for its Byzantine hallways and dusty rooms.

FORMS OF WORSHIP

Although the country of P_____ may have appeared to be like any other tropical country, there were in fact a few significant differences.

For one thing, I discovered not long after my arrival that the people worshipped candles. The large white candles decorated all the churches, and people paid their last *centavo* to light these candles, and the *centavos* were hauled away in large iron strongboxes, to be counted at the back of the churches by priests with long, pale fingers and shiny, polished nails.

The air was filled with a certain tang, as of wood smoke. It had a brownish pallor. The people were very dark. They were much given to perspiration.

The prevalence of candles was blamed for the poor air quality. Studies were done, in the most renowned universities of the land, studies involving numerous beakers of air, in all gradations of brown.

The scientists declared, "The air is bad. This bad air–we must somehow get rid of it."

No one knew how to accomplish this. They thought if they blew very hard, some of this bad air might be blown right out of the country and into the middle of the Pacific Ocean. But no one had breath that was strong enough. The brown air stayed where it was.

GEOGRAPHICAL FEATURES

For a country of its size, P_____ had an astonishing number of volcanoes. These volcanoes were of all heights and widths. Some were short and squat, and others were tall and perfectly cone-shaped. Some were in the middle of lakes, and their deep, dark cones held a terrifying allure, for time after time the most intrepid divers attempted to explore these depths, only to disappear forever.

There were also volcanoes that were so flat that people had even forgotten they were volcanoes and planted fields of rice, corn, and tobacco over them.

Now and then, one of these flat volcanoes would rise up and terrorize the populace with its unexpected fury. Then a cascade of heavy gray sludge poured down onto the fields, and the people left their homes in disarray. This happened about once every hundred years. So the people grew complacent and decided that they could put up with the inconvenience of not knowing whether the ground hid a volcano. And every hundred years, they were surprised. And every hundred years, farms were buried and a few people died.

In connection with this, it is worthwhile to mention the classic work of the Spanish friar Lucretio Andalucia Sevilla (1759 - 1821) *De terrae motu* (On the Motion of the Earth), inspired by the destructive earthquake which struck the town of Lucban in 1800 or 1801. The adjoining towns of Bacolor and Lubao were buried by volcanic ashes in 1818, by the further explosion of two flat volcanoes hitherto buried in a rice field. This disaster was described by the historian Artemiso de Villacrucis (1810-1888) who wrote the first scientific reports of a volcanic eruption in the archipelago.

There were two such occurrences during my time in P_____ _____, one in 19___ which obliterated the town of L____ and its entire population of 800 souls; and another which was followed by an earthquake so tremendous that the the aftershocks were felt as far away as Indonesia.

From my interviews with the residents of P_____, I was able to deduce the timing of several of the more recent earthquakes, to wit:

July 16, 19___:R____ province, Magnitude 7.7
August 17, 19___:Moro Gulf, of the island of M_____, Magnitude: 7.9
April 7, 19___:Baler, Q_____ province, Magnitude 7.3

One volcano in particular, whose cone was admired by the populace for its perfection, had reportedly erupted 44 times since 1616. Another volcano, this one lying underneath the waters of S___ Lake, had reportedly erupted 33 times since 1572, of which times the most destructive was the earthquake of 1754 (the year of Henry Fielding's death, and the year of birth of Louis XVI, Captain William Bligh, and Charles Maurice de Talleyrand).

Popular lore has it that during this earthquake, the lake water bubbled and boiled, as though it were a seething cauldron. Fish were flung up in huge quantities on the lakeshore. Ash darkened the sky for almost a year. Great fissures opened in the ground with predictable consequences. The effects of this horror can still be seen in the eyes of the people today.

A smaller volcano which residents refer to as Hibok-Hibok had minor activity—no more than a hiccup—in the months before my arrival, the last of which resulted in an avalanche which killed more than 3,000 souls.

In the city of B_____, little more than the dome and belfry of the San G_____ Roman Catholic church remain visible and its handful of remaining parishioners now enter through the window of the choir loft for services. To the eyes of a casual observer, it is as if the surface of the earth around the town had turned itself inside out. This new landscape, as deep as 90 feet, is made up of volcanic ejecta, sand and feather-light pebbles and porous boulders from deep inside the mountain. Vast amounts of the dry material still cover the mountain's slopes, its temperature still up to 495 degrees. When the monsoon torrents come each autumn, the material mixes with the water and begins to flow like concrete pouring from a delivery truck, as much as 30 million cubic yards at a time and as fast as 25 miles an hour.

The people shrug off such occurrences with seeming equanimity.

A TRIP TO THE VOLCANO AT324-03

The letter from my good friend V_____ informed me that it was of the utmost importance that I go to this volcano, as the slopes held a most distinct form of plant life that could not be found anywhere on the archipelago. In damp ravines by the volcanic crater, wrote V_____, there grew a slender, prostrate plant with branched stems and unusual, oblong leaves. These leaves were sheathed with long, soft, brownish hairs, such as those to be found on the arms of a young girl.

I estimated that the distance to the volcano was approximately a day's hike. Consequently, early the next morning I packed my rucksack with several canteens of water, a few packets of dried mango and a pack of cigarettes, and set off.

This volcano lies on the border between the provinces of Z_____ and P_____. Its eruption, midway through the last century, was a devastating calamity, displacing hundreds of thousands of the natives, who fled down the river of A_____ with only the clothes on their backs.

Now it is quiescent, strangely beautiful, with its topmost cone (still perfect, after the eruption) wreathed in clouds.

As is customary in these parts, I was greeted at the foot of the volcano by the local community elder, a man by the name of A_____.

"Welcome!" A_____ declared. His lined features glistened in the rain. He was dark and his body seemed somehow part of the mountain itself, as it reared its bulk into the heavens, behind him. He raised his right hand in a gesture that I could only interpret as: "You come in peace, I welcome you in peace."

Small children danced about in the rain, half-naked. Their mothers watched indulgently from the doorways of a few shacks.

It had taken me more than two hours to hike up the slippery trail, gracelessly stumbling into the mud quite a number of times. Thus disheveled and mud-spattered, I arrived at the village of *Lupang Pangako,* a name which I am told means "Promised Land".

Early the next morning, while I was still lying on my thin pallet, I saw a face appear at the narrow doorway. This face was small and wizened, and I could not tell whether it belonged to a man or a woman. It turned out that the owner of the face was named Florante (a very popular name for men in this country; I am told it comes from the hero of an old heroic epic). He was the village folk healer and had heard about the man who had come to study plants. He had brought with him dried leaves, herbs, and roots which he proceeded to strew around my pallet, in a large circle. I asked him what he was doing, as best I could (though my knowledge of the local dialect is extremely rudimentary). Florante replied that he was cleansing my soul of bad elements, which he could see resting on my brow. I then told him to leave me alone.

He explained that my presence in the village was disturbing to the *Anito*. I had heard this word before, and as best I can surmise, it refers to the gods of the forest, who reside in the rocks and streams.

I walked gingerly, having breakfasted on boiled bananas, yam, an ear of corn and virtually unable to resist the importuning of *Ka* A_____'s family to load up on more fresh bananas. Dusk caught me by a small path where a boy of about seven was tying together a huge bundle of twigs. He got up and motioned me to follow him. I shook my head. For a moment I watched as he disappeared into the deepening gloom and then, seized by I know not what impulse, I took off after him.

He stopped in a clearing where there was a small hut made of dried grass, apparently his residence.

We were silent for a long time as the rain turned into a drizzle ... What thoughts whirled through his mind, I wondered ... How had life been in their former home before the volcano's awakening after 600 years of sleep?

The boy's face was flat and smooth, flat as a sheet of glass. His eyes glistened, as if from something other than the rain. His skin was the color of river water, when it approaches the shore. Before it grew completely dark, I took my leave of him. He began to hum pleasantly as I turned my back. I could hear his humming a good part of my way down to the lowlands.

I have been to the volcano many more times since, with side trips to the streams of I__ on several occasions, but I have never felt the sense of peace I did then.

I found the trek down less arduous than the ascent, although my knees stiffened each time I attempted to slow my descent. When I reached the beach at the mouth to my valley, the breakers were gentle and I lay on my back, allowing the sea to cradle me on its languid arms. My mind emptied. For this one day, in that place, I knew happiness.

SYMBIOSIS

In P_____, as in all countries, there was a ruling class. But the rulers of P_____ were more than extraordinarily dependent on a lower class. And the lower class liked very much to go to the movies. Consequently, the movie stars–the male ones, at least–became the ruling class.

These movies were generally of very poor quality. Curiously, the female stars were named after American soft drinks: they had names like Pepsi and Sarsi, and they liked to take all their clothes off. Later, Pepsi hung herself, and Sarsi went mad. No one knew what happened to them and after a few years, no one even remembered them.

One movie star became very famous for his roles as an aggressive policeman. He was always karate-chopping a gang of robbers or mowing down thugs with an Armalite. He is now the president of the country. The people have a special name for him: only two syllables. They don't bother calling him "Mr. President." They know him by the two-syllable name. Such a country!

THE SKULLS

In P_____, the death penalty was imposed frequently, even for minor offenses. A large majority of the criminals in the jails were of the lower classes.

Executions were always carried out at the hour when Christ uttered the famous words: "My God, my God, why have you forsaken me?" That is to say, at three o'clock in the afternoon. A priest was always present to recite the last rites over the unfortunate.

Once, on my excursions around the capital city, I stumbled upon a cave buried deep in an ancient hillside. The entrance to the cave was well concealed by thick vegetation; it was by the merest chance that I stumbled on it.

Within I found a heap of human bones, among which there were forty-four skulls. Here also I found a head box about 1 meter long which held a row of five or six skulls. The head box was made of a dark wood resembling *molave*, but was in an advanced state of decay. This box had handles carved to represent the head of some animal–possibly a crocodile or a horse.

All of the skulls had an open suture along the median line in the anterior part.

When I told the people of my discovery, they grew very afraid. They shook their heads and crossed themselves. They protested that they were upstanding citizens who practiced the true faith.

ASTROLOGICAL BODIES

It was a strange phenomenon that, in these islands, the moon seemed very close to the earth. Sometimes it seemed to be resting on top of a banana palm. The people came to believe that a part of the moon became trapped in the heart of the palm. I was told by a very old woman that if you chopped down this palm and cut down to its very heart, you found a whitish flesh, firm and sweet. It was a much-prized delicacy.

The moon loomed large. Wherever you stood, in whatever part of the country, you looked up and you saw it.

The people made up stories about the moon. They said she was a beautiful maiden who had been punished and put up in the sky by a vengeful god named B_____. No one knew what her crime was.

Vengeful gods are always punishing beautiful maidens.

The people loved to tell stories.

They also liked to tell stories about mountains. My favorite was the one about Mount M_____. The lady who lived on the mountain was said to be famous for handing out plates of silver and gold to travelers who stumbled across her little grass hut in the jungle. No one knew why she had so many gold and silver plates in the middle of the jungle. Or why she lived in a grass hut. The grass hut was sometimes a palace. It was a very confusing story. Nevertheless, I enjoyed it immensely.

OTHER COUNTRIES

Now, I suggest you compare this country to others. Preferably, to other countries lying at or near the Equator.

Is not this wonderful, hallucinatory country truly unique and blessed– in its mineral-laden soil, its effluvia of life, its swarming multitudes of begging children, its executions carried out so promptly at three o'clock every afternoon?

This is a marvelous country. There is no other on God's earth like it. It is like–what shall I call it? A mote in God's eye.

NOTE: The writer disclaims any pretense to special training in ethnology. He has set down his observations in the hope that qualified persons may become interested enough to make further investigations.

PICTURE

She's leaning forward, as if to kiss him. There's a mark on his cheek; perhaps she's done it already. They are both smiling.

These were my parents in Manila, circa 1956. They were happy; they had always been happy. The happiness of their marriage was like a reproach.

I didn't think he looked that ugly. *"La unica problema es que no es guapo."* Who said this? My grandmother's cousin, Lola Paching. This, at least, was the family story.

But there was a certain kind of attractiveness in my father's face. My mother, I saw now, looked like me. Or like I might have looked if I, too, had been happy. She was wearing a white scoop-necked gown. Her breasts looked heavy and full, but her arms were thin. She was looking up at my father and smiling.

I am collecting old pictures now. I don't know what this tells me about this stage of my life.

My husband and two children are far away. My husband said, as he packed their things, *Don't call us. We're happier that way.* I may have murmured something in reply, compulsively polite, even under such circumstances. I didn't know whether I meant to say, Good Riddance. Or, I'll be seeing you. Or, have a pleasant day! I stood on the driveway and gave a little wave as I watched my two children's faces, grave in the back seat.

Marco is 10; his sister, Maya, is 4. I had them long ago, when I was a different person. Now I find it hard to remember who that person was, who changed their diapers without complaint, who gave them heated milk in the middle of the night. They lived in a neat house then.

Two nights ago, my sister-in-law called from the Philippines. The phone sounded shrill in the empty house.

"And how are you?" she asked. It seemed to me that she rolled her r's unnecessarily.

"Fine," I said, and decided to say nothing about my husband

leaving.

My sister-in-law knew already, but pretended she didn't. Instead, she asked me a string of leading questions, and I deflected them all by saying, "Ben is not here right now. He took the children for some ice cream."

I'd been gardening, and my hands were muddy. I looked at my black-rimmed nails as I sat cradling the phone against my ear. Uh-huh, uh-huh, uh-huh, I said, not really sure what my sister-in-law was saying. The sound of her words was like a stream, the words indistinguishable from one another.

Finally I said, "And how is dad? Is he all right?"

"Fine, he's fine," my sister-in-law said. Abruptly, she said she had to go. I heard the line go dead. I sat there, the receiver in my hand. After a long while, I stood up and decided to get myself a drink.

But the refrigerator was empty. It seemed my husband had taken even the last two beer bottles that had been on the top shelf. There was a mess of soggy lettuce in the vegetable crisper, moldy salami in the meat bin. A smell of spoiled milk wafted from the refrigerator shelves.

I went to the bed and lay down. What, what, what would I do now? There was the telephone, black and still. It refused to speak to me. And anyway, when it did speak, it was always my sister-in-law or a solicitor or someone else I didn't want to hear from. No one nice, like my mother or my brothers in the Philippines. Or even my uncle or cousins in Daly City. I got up and thought: I'll hide it. There was a plastic garbage can in the living room. I took the phone and put it there. I didn't unplug it yet, though. I might want to hear the sound of it ringing.

The first night, I watched an old Douglas Fairbanks movie: The Thief of Baghdad. The hero had black-rimmed eyes. Ha, ha. I laughed and laughed. Everything about him was side-splittingly funny. I thought: tomorrow I will go to the video store and rent this film. The sound of my laughter was deep and throaty, and I realized this was one more thing that was changing, along with everything else.

After a long while–two weeks–I got tired of watching old

movies and eating moldy salami. It seemed to me that I should pull myself together. I should at least let my mother in the Philippines know what had happened. I didn't know where my two children were, but that was all right; their father would take care of them. They clung to him, I noticed, as they walked out the door.

"I love you," I had said, and the boy turned his head, but only a little.

"What's that?" I said, thinking he had said something.

"What?" my husband said, turning to face me.

"Nothing, nothing," my son said. He was in a hurry. "Dad's leaving," he said, shrugging his shoulders apologetically before hurrying away.

I watched his legs–skinny brown legs–in their too-large sneakers go stumbling down the front walk. My little girl clutched her father's hand. I couldn't see her face. Then, oh God! I thought. I suddenly wanted to scream. But the neighbors, the neighbors, I thought! And at that moment of indecision, of terrible longing, the children got into the car and zoomed away. I remained standing on the sidewalk, my hands clasped together, watching the car round the corner.

The first days alone in the house, I thought I heard voices: when I was in the garden, when I was lying in bed. I thought I would hear a voice calling, "Ma?" And I would answer to the house, to its shuttered windows. The house breathed back its silent, moldy spaces at me.

The window frames, I noticed, were warped. The picture frames hung crookedly on the walls. Now and then, if I happened to think of it, I would straighten one or two and step back, judging the effect.

In the hallway were a long row of framed prints of Old Manila. These prints depicted 18th century scenes; the plaza in front of the Dominican convent in Intramuros, strangely devoid of people; a view of the Pasig River, crowded with boats. The borders were red; the frames gilt. Why were they here, hanging in the dim upstairs hallway, where no one, not a single guest to our house, could see them?

Eventually I thought: I will adopt a new family. It's easy: all I need to do is advertise. So I took out the *El Cerritos Weekly* and looked in the classifieds. And before I'd turned more than a few pages, I saw it: a picture of a smiling little boy, about seven or eight years old, and Filipino, too, from the looks of him. Underneath the picture was the caption: WILL YOU FEED ME?

Sure! I said! Sure, little boy! I'll bring you to the land of milk and honey, where you'll never ever have to scrounge around in garbage cans ever again. Not if I can help it.

And I didn't know why, but looking at that picture brought a terrible pain to my chest, so that I couldn't rest until I'd gone to the store and bought paper and pen and stamps to write to the boy. And all that night, I tossed and turned, waiting for the mailman to come so that I could run right out and give him the letter, the letter for the little boy. And then I took all my son's things, the old toys he'd left behind in his room because they were too old or too broken or too dirty, and I arranged them in a neat row on the floor and said, "These will be for you, little boy. Come home soon!"

And every night after that I sat looking out the window at the empty street, expecting to see a thin shadow come running up the front walk, a shadow that hopped and skipped, the way my son used to do, when he'd run home in the evenings from a day spent playing in the park or at a friend's house.

In the evenings, there was a strange kind of knocking sound from a corner of one of the eaves facing the side yard. And eventually, after sitting and listening to the sound for what seemed like hours on end, I took the aluminum ladder from the garage–my husband had not taken everything–and leaned it against the side of the house. I climbed gingerly, carefully, and there, in a corner of a rain spout gutted with dark brown leaves was a fat green toad. It looked at me mildly, with its yellow eyes.

"Oh, you poor frog. You poor, poor frog," I said. As I said it, there was again that ache in my chest, an ache which was rapidly becoming familiar, as familiar as the sound of my shallow breathing when I lay in bed at night, waiting for sleep. Cupping the toad carefully in my right hand, I backed down the ladder. It sat still. Its skin was slimy and cold. I could feel the pulse in its throat against my fingers.

I thought, I will put it in the children's terrarium. Then I looked and looked for this, but it was nowhere to be found. Standing in the middle of the dimly lit garage, I began to wonder: could they have taken that, too? I hadn't known it had meant so much to them. For years it had sat on a high shelf in the garage, after their last lizard had died. The one named Ed.

And still I wandered about, with the toad cupped in the palm of my right hand. I couldn't put it down. The beat of its heart reminded me of other things, things unconnected to my present life. A baby underneath my ribs. The rip and tear between my legs. The smell of soap.

Think, think, think, I said. Did I happen to sell it during our last garage sale? Was it in the batch I sent off to the Salvation Army, along with the crib and the other baby things? The truck came yesterday: a powerfully built black man had approached the door. He said nothing as he carted the stuff away. There goes my life, I wanted to say.

I watched him fling the clothes into the back of the truck. The truck lumbered slowly down the street, and at the second corner made a slow right turn.

I put the toad in the bathtub. Its color seemed muted and muddy against the white enamel. I remembered leaning my daughter over the edge of the tub, washing her hair. The long black strands of it. Now the toad gazed up at me, not moving.

Things were happening to me now, in that house. First, the water stopped. The toilet began to give off a smell. My hair stood up stiff and straight from my forehead, and I was surprised, really surprised, to see so many strands flecked with white. If I turned my head to one side, I could also see bare patches of skull above each ear. The hair fell down the sink—where else could it go? And the water moved sluggishly down the drain.

Now, when the mailman came up the walk, I ran anxiously

to the front door to greet him. Wordlessly, he would hand me the pile of supermarket flyers and turn his back. He was Asian—perhaps Chinese or Vietnamese. He didn't seem to understand English. His steps seemed to quicken as he left the front porch.

The letter for the little boy lay forgotten by the door. I looked at it with indifference after the mailman had disappeared.

One sunny day, I decided to take a walk around the block. I put on shorts, a T-shirt, my favorite sandals. I noticed the wisteria in bloom at the corner of the front porch. I saw the top of Mrs. Olson's head, behind a tall hedge; she was mowing her lawn, stopping every now and then. I dragged myself along. I couldn't move without breathing heavily. The hair stood up wildly from the top of my head. The bald patches at the side of my skull stared up at the sun.

I stopped dead in my tracks. At that moment, the street was wide and empty. There was a tall house with a brick front directly in front of me. The shutters were drawn at all the windows and a large black dog glared at me from behind the iron gate. Had that family always had a dog? It seemed I had never noticed it, or even the iron gate, before.

I was struck dumb. I felt, this is the way it will be forever: me, the empty street, the endless sun.

LENOX HILL, DECEMBER 1991

I would have liked to say: I took the first plane to New York, but I did not. I am ashamed to say it, but I didn't at first believe my brother-in-law when he called and said my sister was very sick. I remember listening to his foreign, English voice, and a host of memories came over me—memories of other times, other crises and emergencies, times that left me feeling helpless and angry. And he sounded so matter-of-fact, so *English* and above it all, and when he said she had strep I thought: Now you are really pulling my leg, you say all these awful things are happening and she has *strep?* I had wanted to hang up on him, but did not, and the rest of that day I busied myself with office work and did not think about my sister anymore.

We lived on opposite coasts; when my sister and I first came to America, she chose to settle on the East Coast, I on the West. I had always thought of her as more adventurous, more self-confident, tough. I wanted to be close to my mother's relatives, who lived in various San Francisco suburbs.

I had seen my sister only once in the last three years. She was busy with her job in a big bank, with her three children and her busy family. Sometimes I liked to imagine her life: my sister in a dark suit, walking quickly down the busy avenues of Manhattan. I had seen pictures of her in a mink coat, standing in front of an imposing gray building that I thought must be her bank. I had heard her talk of attending auctions at Sotheby's.

It was a Dr. Sterling who called the house, early on the morning of my sister's third day in the hospital. He said: Come as soon as you can, there's not much time.

My aunt drove me to the airport. I asked for a seat by the window and curled up with my legs tucked under me. Strong sunlight filled the airplane cabin. It was impossible to sleep. I looked down and saw clouds; a mountain; a river snaking through brown canyons. Throughout the long flight I read passages from the book I happened to check out of the library the previous week: *The Four Winds: A Shaman's Journey Into the Amazon*. It was written by two men, Erik Jendresen and Alberto Villoldo, but it was really Villoldo's story, Villoldo's journey to the Amazon. In the early section of the book, I came across a passage about an autopsy: the corpse was that of a 37-year-old woman, and as he watches a medical student put a piece of her brain on a slide, Villoldo asks himself, Where is the consciousness that was Jennifer, where were her memories, the unique trace that had made her who she was?

When I arrived in New York, it was late at night. Strange men held up signs near the baggage carousels, and I was frightened and tried to get away from them, but one of them spotted me and asked me if I needed a limousine. Yes! I said, But I will not ride alone with you. I must have seemed hysterical. He looked at me carefully and then said, Wait here, I will find someone to share the ride.

After what seemed like an interminable wait, he returned with a young student: a Korean visiting friends at Columbia. The Korean talked and talked, all the way into Manhattan. I think we passed a bridge and entered a tunnel. With startling suddenness we were in the middle of canyons of buildings. The driver dropped off the Korean and we began to talk. He was a young black man, with two children, and he told me he had been waiting at the airport for hours, and he was hungry and wanted to go home and have his dinner. He didn't charge me very much. I was sorry when I got out of the limousine.

This is the part where things become difficult. I have to switch to another way of writing about events, in order to get through the rest of what happens. I can describe things more accurately if I present, briefly, scenes that stand out in my mind, as of—

Memory 1: Arrival

I am at the apartment on Park Avenue. It must be after 10

at night. All the lights in the apartment are blazing, and my
sister's two older children, aged five and four, are wide awake.
My first impression upon walking in the door is of loud screams
and an atmosphere of general hubbub and disorder. My brother-
in-law walks up, holding his youngest, only six months old, in
his arms.

It is the first time I have seen this fabled place, this place
that all my sister's classmates in Manila know to visit when
they are in New York. And now I note the mirrored hallway,
the high-ceilinged kitchen with its capacious island, the various
suites of rooms. I ask for my mother and with barely a word
my brother-in-law relieves me of my bag and directs me to the
hospital. I go out into a night which is much warmer than I had
come to expect. All up and down Park Avenue, an amazing
sight: Christmas trees are blinking bravely in the darkness. I
pass lighted doorways, behind which stand doormen with surly
faces. I pass women in fur coats walking their dogs. I do not
feel the cold.

Memory 2: Lenox Hill

I am at the intensive care ward. There, at the end of a long
row of beds, I see a swollen shape, lying with legs awkwardly
spread-eagled. Long, thick black hair is spread out on a pillow.
I instinctively head towards this head of black hair, and pass
beds filled with old, old people, some with their hospital gowns
pushed all the way up to their stomachs, revealing bone-thin limbs.
Some with their mouths twisted open, as though gasping for air.
I at first do not believe this swollen body I am approaching to
be my sister's, but when I come close and see my mother there,
my heart fills with grief, a grief so great I want to shout over
and over: WHAT HAVE THEY DONE TO YOU?

My mother looks up at me, and whatever I prepared myself
to find when I arrived at the hospital, it certainly wasn't this:
my mother looks at me, and her face is happy and peaceful.
"Come," she says, sensing my fear, coaxing me forward. She is

strength, strength itself, sitting there in the intensive care ward, while all my insides seem in danger of cracking open, and something cold snakes into my heart.

I look into my sister's eyes: they are flaming red and twice the normal size. A thick, opaque film of fluid coats them and oozes out at the corners. Her swollen hand makes a faint movement toward the ventilator in her mouth.

This is what my sister has: three IVs, one in each arm to push drugs and fluids, an arterial line in her left arm to draw blood and for hooking up to a transducer for constant blood pressure readings; a nasogastric tube running through her nose and into her stomach, hooked up to a suction machine on the floor to drain her stomach constantly so that she won't aspirate, regurgitate into her trachea; an endotracheal tube down her throat; a ventilator because she can't breathe by herself. Whenever she moves her tongue the monitor emits a faint beep.

I grab her limp hand, knowing that now she cannot pull away, as she would have done were she not so seriously ill. I sob, because I realize this is something I had not been able to do for many years, and it has to be now, now in these circumstances. I sob, too, because my sister, who I had always remembered as a rather vain person, who when she was 16 had had a nose job and an eye job and various other things done to make her look less Oriental, who was thirty-four and had three young children, was no more, and this new physical reality, this shape that allowed me to hold her hand without resistance, had taken her place.

Now there is a flurry of beeps from the ventilator. My mother bends forward and tells my sister not to talk. My mother tells her, "There will be plenty of time later." But my sister is still biting down, moving her tongue. Nurses hurry over. The beeps increase. I feel something terrible is happening, and whatever it is I feel I must be the cause. I step back from the bed while the nurses call out, "Cecilia, Cecilia, stop biting the ventilator. Stop it!" I can not bear to hear my sister addressed in such a way, as though she were a five-year-old. She is helpless, she cannot move. If she were able to, she might flail away at one of these nurses, but now she can only lie there, her tongue perhaps the only part of her capable of movement.

I want to shout: "Can't you let her speak? Can't you get the ventilator out of her mouth?" Because I can see how it hurts her: that monstrous thing, pushing her swollen tongue to the inside of her cheek, pressing on her cracked lips. But I stand there, dumb. Already there are at least two other nurses there, hurrying, hurrying, preparing to inject my sister with a sedative. I do nothing. Instead I flee from them and head for the waiting lounge, cursing my cowardice.

Memory 3: The Waiting Lounge

It is a tiny room with two lumpy, plastic-covered sofas in a sick shade of avocado green, and a window that overlooks a side street and some brownstone buildings. Against one wall is a pay phone, and newspapers are scattered on a coffee table. Later I will come to know every particular of this room: the squares of graying linoleum, the exact depressions on the sofa cushions, the coffee rings on the cheap wooden tables, the television suspended by a steel arm from the wall. I will cradle the phone receiver against my ear and make numerous, teary calls to California, to my husband. My mother and I will sit on the green sofa and wait for the doctor to tell us about my sister's latest blood gas readings, minute improvements in her lung capacity. We will sit here and pace and get to know the relatives of Mrs. Beatrice Sulkin–a son, a daughter, a husband–who pace with us. We will come to know all this.

Memory 4: Filipina Nurses

Two of them come to me as I sob on the sofa and one of them hands me a box of tissues. "*Calma lang,*" she says. Her companion says, "Don't worry. She is much better now. She was very bad this morning."

Their words comfort me but I continue to sob, though I realize it is now more for myself than for my sister–sobbing because the long trip in the airplane, the leave-taking from my son and husband this Christmas, was so very hard, and because I am exhausted. *"Calma lang."*

A young Filipina named Lourdes is her nurse that first night. She is pretty, with thick black hair plaited and fastened up at the back of her head. She jokes with the young interns, and keeps injecting my sister with Benadryl. Lourdes tells me that my sister keeps fighting the ventilator. She tells me that earlier they had to strap her down to the bed. I had noticed the purplish marks on her wrists and ankles and wondered where they came from. Tuesday morning, two days earlier, was when they had almost lost her. It was the night my brother-in-law had gone home to spend some time with the children.

They said she was thrashing in the bed. Perhaps it wasn't fear so much as the feeling that she was drowning, her lungs filling up with fluid. But the thrashing was using up whatever little oxygen was going to her brain. And they had to strap her down.

Since my mother arrived, Thursday morning, she has been quiet. She looks at my mother, and she knows her. My mother strokes her hair tenderly. Tenderly she fans my sister's legs and pushes up the hospital gown because my sister needs air. She needs air more than anything in the world. Look at her fingers and toes, already turning blue ...

Memory 5: Doctors

It may be the third or fourth day, and I am already feeling how ineffectual my presence is. I am standing by my sister's bed, but I don't–can't–speak. I stand, dumb with misery, by my sister's hospital bed.

The doctors have injected her with Pavulon, a paralyzing agent. They say they had to sedate her because anxiety increases the heart rate and uses up oxygen and they are worried she might suffer brain damage. They say she can still hear. I ask them, what is it like, this hearing? They tell me, like hearing voices in your sleep. Yet I hesitate to speak to my sister in the same loud voice the nurses use: Cecilia, I'm going to put eye patches on you now; Cecilia, I'm going to put drops in your eyes. I stand there, dumb with misery.

Memory 6: My Uncle

I am jealous of my mother's younger brother because he has managed to make my sister giggle. It is the last time we see her conscious and awake. He takes one of her swollen feet and starts to tickle it. My sister's shoulders rise and her swollen mouth parts and even with the ventilator in her mouth she does look strangely happy. I watch, dumb with misery.

Later, I try to tell her things. My voice is soft. I can think of nothing to say. Only things like, "Chinggay," using the name I much prefer to her Christian name, "I am here." Here! But what does that mean, exactly? Even my touch is light and tentative. I am unable to stroke her arms with my mother's vehemence, my brother-in-law's vigor. They seize the parts of her body as though claiming her, inciting her to struggle. But I am afraid.

Memory 7: Sunday Night

My mother and I are stretched out, one to a sofa, in the tiny waiting room. It feels as though we have just fallen asleep when someone comes in and switches on the light. My mother and I are up instantly. It is the young doctor, Dr. Rosen, wearing green scrubs. He gives us my sister's latest blood gas count. He is ecstatic. We are, too. We think now that my sister will surely live.

Memory 8: In the Kitchen

In this bright place, all white tile and chrome appliances, I sit on a high stool and tell my brother-in-law about my sister's latest blood gas reading. He is happy but trying hard not to lose control. I tease him that he should take my sister on a long cruise for their tenth anniversary, which is coming up in May. He tells me they have planned to go to Egypt.

Memory 9: Monday

I spend the whole day away from the hospital. I feel light-headed and happy. I walk down Fifth Avenue and marvel at the giant golden snowflakes strung across the street. When I finally check back at the hospital, it is late at night. My mother is at her customary place, but her head is bowed. Poor woman, I think. She must be exhausted. But when she looks up, the expression on her face frightens me and I ask, what is it, what is it? The ventilator, she says. They tried to take her off it today, but she had a setback. A terrible setback. Her body just couldn't take it.

Memory 10: Doormen

I begin to look forward to the walks in the cold, and know buildings and doormen. I know all the doormen in my sister's building. One in particular, an old man named George, is very kind. He is the one who runs after me if I happen to get into the elevator without speaking to him and asks: "How is she?" My chin pressed down into my overcoat, I invariably shake my head and say, "Not good." George lifts his hands, shrugs his shoulders. "It's in God's hands," he says.

Memory 11: Other People

I sit on a sagging chair in the foyer. It is 3, 4 in the morning. I sit and look out the window and wait for it to get light. In the room behind me, a doctor is shouting into a phone: Are you crazy? What do you think I am, stupid? And she goes on and on like that, interminably.

There is someone else with a terrible cough. Choking on phlegm. It is an old man or an old woman. I want to cover my ears, to shout: Stop it! Stop it!

I am alone, waiting for my mother to come. Waiting for my brother-in-law. I am tired. Who are all these strangers yakking in the foyer?

Hours later, I walk past the rows of sick old people, being careful to keep my eyes down. I see my sister lying there, her bloated shape, her eyes taped shut, no sign of life or movement. There is no one with her. The children's nanny, a Filipina who has left her two young boys with her mother so she can come to America and care for my sister's children, was supposed to have been there at 10. It is now almost 11. Not even my brother-in-law is there.

Memory 12: Tuesday

My sister has a bad night. In fact, we nearly lose her. My mother rushes to the apartment to get me. It is cold and raining. In her panic, she slips and hurts her knee. The wound has bled through her pants when she arrives at the apartment, but she immediately rushes back with me to the hospital without bothering to change. When we arrive at the hospital, I am annoyed to see that the nurse on duty, an elderly Filipina, is wandering aimlessly around with a nonchalant air, as though nothing is happening. "She is all right now, she is stable," she keeps telling my distraught mother. Stable, but only for the moment, I think bitterly.

Memory 13: Mary Ellen

I do not recognize the nurse, though thank God it is not the other one of last night, the old Filipina who seemed only to want to sit down and smoke her cigarette in the waiting room and read the newspapers scattered on the floor.

Mary Ellen looks Irish. She has red hair, calm gray eyes, a wide mouth that seems always on the verge of saying something sarcastic. To all my queries of "How is she?" she has only one answer: "The same." But I like this nurse, with her warm, stolid, squarish body, and her clean smell. I think to myself: my sister will not die as long as she is there.

When her shift is over, I want to tell her: come back soon. I watch her leave the ward in her going-out clothes. She and another nurse, another Filipina, are heading for the elevators, and they look different, almost coquettish, in short skirts and sheer black stockings. I wander back alone to my sister's bed.

Memory 14: Wednesday

My sister is no longer the only young woman in the intensive care ward. Everyone seems to be gathered around the latest arrival: a woman who has been placed in Bed No. 1, closest to the nurses' station. I watch them wheel her in and, in my confused state, mistake her black hair for my sister's. I go to my sister's bedside, but I cannot sit down. Someone has taken away the chair.

Beside her someone has placed a small pocketbook: *Furrow*, the collected writings of Jose Maria Escriva, the founder of Opus Dei. He is about to be beatified and Mrs. Yuzon who works in my office tells me the period just before his beatification is when prayers to him have the most potency. On the window sill my brother-in-law has propped up a picture of Clarissa and Franco, sitting on Santa Claus' lap.

Memory 15: The Pay Phone

The pay phone in the waiting room rings annoyingly. Hello, a young woman says. Can I speak to Mrs. Greenfeld? There is no Mrs. Greenfeld here, I say. I hang up. Not five minutes later, it rings again. I know there is a Mrs. Greenfeld there, with

Mr. Weinberger. What am I? An answering service? I go to call someone. A young male intern comes to the phone. No, no, he says, and hangs up. Ten minutes later, the phone rings again. Please, says the young woman. I need to speak to my mother. I know she is there: a Mrs. Greenfeld who is with Mr. Weinberger. I go back to the ward. There, next to Bed No. 2, is a forty-ish woman in a tweed overcoat and a slouchy hat. Are you Mrs. Greenfeld? I ask. Yes, she says. Mr. Weinberger looks very pale, and his mouth is twisted in a kind of grimace. You have a phone call, I say. She comes to the phone and I can hear rapid-fire Yiddish and I know that somewhere in there is some mention about me and the number of times I have hung up on the daughter saying, There is no Mrs. Greenfeld here.

I collect my things and go back to the apartment. There is no one in the study. I lie down on the leather couch. I look out and see it has begun to snow. The phone keeps ringing: someone called Donna Lopez from Washington, D.C.; Brandon Howard, my sister's boss at Chemical Bank; Jake, a friend of my brother-in-law from Merrill Lynch.

I see Clarissa and Franco playing outside in the hallway with the chocolate egg I had given them as a Christmas present. Clarissa has black hair, and Franco is blond. Clarissa is beautiful, but Franco, with his blond hair and slanted eyes, looks mournful and lost.

The chocolate egg has rolled to one corner and they are fascinated with the wooden box and the synthetic straw, and Clarissa says she will put a little bird in it–a bird with a broken wing. I go with her to her room and I start pretending to cook with her pots and pans. She stares at me at first, with big, round eyes, and then gradually it dawns on her what I am doing and she begins to smile. Then the nanny comes to say my mother has called for me to take her place at the hospital for a while. I am flustered and run out, forgetting about Clarissa. She runs after me, screaming, but her nanny catches her and holds her firmly. I am not going anywhere, the nanny says.

Memory 16: Good-bye

The day my father arrives from the Philippines. No one told me he was coming. I simply enter the intensive care ward early one morning, and he is there. He is wearing a fine, brown cardigan, and his hair is neatly combed. He sits back on a hospital chair, not saying anything. His eyes are dry. He looks essentially the same person as the one who sat at the breakfast table every morning when I was growing up. Yet, how strange it is to see him sitting here, this cold winter morning, with the snowflakes blowing by the half-open window.

I know I have to leave. There are too many people in the apartment, everyone getting on each other's nerves, and Mary Ellen has told me that my sister can continue in her present state for a long, long time. I go to the hospital alone and see my sister lying on the bed, inert, her eyes taped shut. I look at her cracked, swollen lips and jowls, her bluish fingers and toes, trying to fix her image in my mind. I am anxious when I see that she is alone again, no one there to massage her limbs or comb her hair. The nurses are busy with other patients and leave me alone. I stand there for a long time, simply watching. Now is the time, I think. Now is the time to tell her what she has meant to me, and how much I love her. I see her shudder, a movement I have observed before and which had distressed me until my mother said, "She is coughing." Now she coughs, and coughs some more. Her hand moves up slightly toward her stomach, but it is a half-gesture. Before the motion can be completed, the hand sinks down again, and she is still.

"I love you," I say, with all the strength I can muster, but the sound comes out small, almost inaudible. I stand there, immobilized. I want to kiss her, but dare not. I remember the doctor's words: "The next 48 hours are crucial. Any little infection could kill her." And I can feel, at the back of my throat, the scratchy beginnings of a cough. And I do not want anything to harm my sister. I do not want any harm to come to her at all.

I say good-bye to Mary Ellen, who is once again her nurse,

and Mary Ellen gives me a tight little smile and her eyes remain detached, though I tell myself she is not unkind.

A few days later, I am at the apartment, packing to return to California, when the phone rings. It is my mother, calling from the hospital. She says the words quietly. My head drops to the table and I realize now that these words were the ones I was expecting to hear. My sobs are shattering and everyone in the apartment comes running and, yes, I want everyone to know it, my sister is no more.

My mother keeps repeating, "To see her in a shroud–" I think of my sister in a winding sheet, on a hospital bed. Later, there is some back and forth on whether or not she should be cremated. I think it is important for my sister's body to be brought back home–important because that is the Filipino way: to have an open casket for nine days, where everyone can come and look and say their farewells. But it is my brother-in-law who objects, and his wish prevails. He does not want his children to see their mother in a casket. She is cremated in New York, and her ashes are flown home to Manila by my mother. My niece, my sister's eldest child, draws a picture–a figure ascending to clouds, and beneath it, she has her father write the words: "My mother goes up to heaven, and leaves behind her bones."

EPILOGUE

In the morgue, there was a toe tag on my sister's right foot. Her hands were bound. She was wrapped in a winding sheet. I asked my mother, "Could you get a piece of her hair for me? To keep?"

My sister was going to be cremated. My mother said, "I want it done quickly." If I hadn't asked my mother this, there would have been nothing, nothing of my sister's to hold on to.

In the morgue, my mother cut locks of my sister's beautiful, long black hair. But not before stroking my sister's hands and noting the traces of mauve nail polish, applied only two weeks before.

"You know," my mother told me later, her voice rising with amazement, "she looked so beautiful. She had gone back to her old size, not that swollen shape she'd been in the hospital, when they were pumping her full of hydrocortisone. I recognized her again."

My mother gave a few strands of hair to me; the rest she kept for herself.

It wasn't until six months later that I could bring myself to open the package from the hospital which contained the autopsy report. It was the end of a hot day. The hills were dry and brown. Voices carried from the outside. I was alone on my deck, in the Santa Cruz Mountains, in the beginning of a dry summer. Hawks circled the pale blue sky. I heard their shrill and mournful cries. The cat hunted in the tall grass below me. Sometimes it would bring me trophies: rabbits; rats; once, a gopher. My son was at camp. My husband hadn't returned from the office. Then, the line that stopped me from reading was the first: *The decedent is initially viewed unclothed.*

I put the report away.

Years later, in September, I found it again, buried underneath a box of old papers. I started to read and found it beautiful, this exploration of my dead sister's body, its description of the wrinkled mucosa of her esophagus, the color of her gastric mucosa identified as "light beige", the yellow-brown of her hepatic artery–all this so much more eloquent than the body they pulled out of a drawer in the morgue to show my mother, when she arrived from taking my sister's children to school. I finger the report's nine pages; examine dates; pore over the doctors' signatures.

I asked a friend, a heart surgeon in Minneapolis, to explain to me the meaning of words like epicardial, extravasated, sub-arachnoid, basilar. She said, send me the report of Case No. M91-9915. I waited, then. Her news came back: "Basically," she told me, "your sister died of heart failure."

In the end, my friend was wrong. It wasn't heart failure: why did she lie? There it is, the words clear as day at the end of the report: sepsis as a result of necrotizing pneumonia.

At the end of the typed descriptions, a handwritten report of a microscopic examination of the brain, written by a Dr. Angelina P. Szper. Angelina!

And there, finally, is the peace I'm looking for: in the frontal lobe, an acute hemorrhage about the necrotic vein; fibrin thrombi in nearby vessels. The splenium: multiple small hemorrhages and infarcts. The cerebellum: scattered acute hemorrhages and necrotic vessels. I want to know this because it tells me that perhaps it was better that my sister died.

The report says that portions of my sister's brain are saved in a stock jar.

INFECTED

It was a disease, their stepmother said. The children came back from Manila, and suddenly they stopped listening to her. They were running around the apartment, infected with restlessness. Pick up your shoes, pick up your clothes, she would tell them. Their father yelled at them. He was a tall, imposing man with a large nose. His glasses slid down and made him look like a strange type of bird.

The eldest, a girl, almost nine, looked at him and thought how strange her father looked standing there, hands clenched. She thought: he doesn't understand. All she wanted were Polly Pockets. Back home in her room in Manila, there were Polly Pockets lined up in rows on shelves that her grandmother had put up for her in her mother's old room. There was also a dollhouse, with a rug that her now-dead mother had made for the miniature living room. There, the girl had her own four-poster canopied bed, and white sheets with eyelet ruffles. The girl would bounce up and down on the bed. Stretched out, looking at the white pillows against the dark wood of the bedposts, she could almost think she was a queen.

In New York, where the children lived, it was starting to get cold. They stood on the street corner, waiting for the school bus, pressed against each other for warmth. The wind blew down the avenue, making their cheeks red. They held each other's hands. When the schoolbus came, they told each other, hurry up, hurry up! They clutched their heavy school satchels. They struggled on to the bus in their bulky coats, their heavy lace-up shoes.

When they got home, their father was angry. Pick up your shoes, he would say over and over. They didn't understand what the thing was about the shoes. The shoes seemed to materialize in the living room, in the hallway, in spite of themselves. Then they would go scurrying around, scooping up the hateful things, the things with the laces that were so hard to tie in the mornings, that always got their fingers in knots just when they needed to be out the door.

The food was different, too. After a summer of eating rice cakes, they didn't want to go back to eating frozen chicken nuggets and fish sticks, which was all the two maids served them because their father and stepmother both worked in a bank and kept late hours, and the maids were lazy when the master and mistress were not at home. It was not just the rice cakes the children missed, but the vegetables boiled in coconut milk, and the garlicky taste of the chicken. Their tongues curled backwards when they looked at the frozen food heated up in the microwave. Their stomachs, distended and full from a diet rich in pork and rice, suddenly seemed to shrivel up and sometimes the New York food would not go down and came back up the wrong way and then the stepmother flew into a passion. I have to be at work, she would say. Do you understand? I have a job! I have to be at work!

So finally their father threatened them. I will never send you back there again, he said. He was English and his parents were always telling him how spoiled his children were. For a week, the children were quiet. The two eldest talked about it and decided they must tiptoe around the apartment, especially when their stepmother was reading.

One evening, their grandmother called from Manila. Their father would not let them talk to her, but they knew it was their grandmother. Their father kept them out of the room and spoke in low, hushed tones. They pressed their ears against the bedroom door, listening. They could imagine their father's head moving up and down, up and down as he talked. That stentorian voice. They liked listening to their grandmother, the way her voice moved up and down, like a pianist practicing scales. She must have been talking about Christmas plans. When they were in Manila for the summer, their grandmother had told them they would be visiting her again at Christmas. But now their father came out of his bedroom and said they were not going to Manila for Christmas; they were going to Mexico. Mexico! Did they know anyone in Mexico? No, their father said. We will stay in a hotel. It will be warm there. We will stay on a beach. Your stepmother needs to relax. This has all been a great strain on her.

The girl grew wild with disappointment. She thought of her aunt, her mother's sister, in San Francisco. She had the telephone number, written down somewhere. Where was it? She searched frantically in all her coat pockets. Her aunt had called one day, when her father was out. She had made the girl write down the number, saying it slowly and carefully, so that the girl could write it down in her laborious script. Now remember, the aunt had said, you must always dial "1" when it's long distance. Remember, always begin with the "1." Her aunt spoke deliberately and slowly, as though it was very very important that the girl understand this.

The girl understood what her aunt was trying to say. Her aunt was worried. The new mother was very thin and had never had children. She was 42, four years older than their father. She was always impatient, complaining whenever the children, scurrying around her, accidentally jostled her or trod on the toes of her high-heeled shoes. She acted as though she were being buffetted by a high wind. Do not come near me, she would yell! Keep away!

Now where was her aunt's number? Because the girl was always forgetting where she put things, and her room was always cluttered with toys that the maids then tossed haphazardly into the corners when it was time to vacuum, this number had vanished and the girl never found it.

The middle boy was always having accidents. He dropped things. He didn't dare tell his father that in Manila, his grandmother rubbed his body with hot oil every night before going to bed. It was the ritual he enjoyed the most. Stretched out naked on the cool sheets, his grandmother rubbed his body and slowly his mind would drift. Very soon, he was asleep. In New York, there was no one to rub his body. He hugged feather pillows. They were too soft and did not feel like the hands of his grandmother. His body sank into them; they were unresisting, inert things. He had nightmares. In the middle of the night, he would cry out. Jesus Christ, his father would yell. Jesus Christ!

The youngest was five. He looked the most like his mother. He had her eyes and her splayed toes. This, at least, was what everyone in Manila told him. He remembered very little about his mother, but he knew he looked like her. There were no pictures of her in the apartment any more, so when he tried to think about his mother, he looked in the mirror. She must have been light-skinned, then, and had a small mouth. The aunt in San Francisco had a mouth with thick, full lips. They had spent a few days with her in the spring. She was always hugging and kissing. "Does your new mother do this?" she asked the little boy once. "No," he said. "Why not?" the aunt said. "I don't know," the child said.

And after that, back in New York, he would observe other mothers with their children: how they held their children's hands; how concern seemed to jump into their faces whenever they shepherded their children across the street. "But I have a mother," he would think.

Before the new mother came, they only had their father. But they had all of him. He would come home from the office, loosen his tie, and, still in his suit, get down on all fours in the playroom. The children would scream with delight. They would hang on to his neck, his shoulders. He didn't care if they pulled at his glasses, or rumpled his clothes. His shoes were all scuffed. But this was their father before. Now that he had married again, he had forgotten how to get down on all fours. Now he was always telling them to behave. At dinnertime, which when their parents were home was a formal meal at which the children had to sit very quietly on the stiff-backed chairs and wait until it was their turn to be served, he seemed weary. The stepmother had a nervous way of looking around. Craning her head this way and that, she would say, where's the salt? What happened to the butter dish? This would send ripples of nervousness through the children. Was the salt under the table? Did one of them put it there? They couldn't remember. Where was the butter dish? What did it look like? Had they even seen it at all? They would look at her, jumpy in their seats. Their stepmother was exasperated. Dinner never went as planned. There was always something going wrong. The children could not behave. Either their elbows would fly out while they were spooning food onto their plates, or something would drop to the floor. Their stepmother would roll her eyes, and their father's face would grow red with embarrassment. Don't you know how to eat? he would say. Sometimes he would send them away. Go to your room, he would say. They jumped up then, feeling a great surge of excitement and joy. But they must not run. They knew this. They tried to walk slowly, carefully, putting one foot in front of the other, until they were all the way down the hallway and into their own section of the apartment. They would fling themselves on their beds. Without talking, they all began thinking of the same thing: the house in Manila, surrounded by mango trees; the swimming pool with its clear blue water; the black dog in the kitchen; the love birds in cages; the smells.

The middle child would get up and start playing with his Sega games. Pow! Pow! Pow! He had Mortal Kombat II. He was Subzero. He was Reptile. He could send snakes shooting out of the palms of his hands. Get down here! The words "Flawless Victory" imprinted on his brain and obliterated the shards of memory.

After a while, the eldest, too, would get up. But she was very listless. She would take up her Barbie dolls, one after the other. They all looked the same: all platinum blonde, with long hair. None of them looked like her. She was dark. Her skin, her hair, and her eyes were dark. People in Manila said she looked like her grandmother. She didn't know what to play with. She wandered aimlessly around the room, touching this and that.

The youngest lay on his bed, sucking his thumb and looking at the ceiling. He didn't tell the others but once, in a park by the

East River, he had seen his old nanny, the one who had been with them when their mother was still alive. At least, he had thought it was her, though when she saw him, and he smiled and waved, she didn't respond. She was pushing a blonde little boy in a stroller. The nanny was from the Philippines, like the children's mother, and for two years after their mother died, and before their father married again, she had taken care of them. But the stepmother did not like her because, she said, the nanny "talked back." So she had sent the nanny away.

The youngest had stared at the nanny, but she was already turning her back. He wanted to bawl but he was afraid of what his sister would say. The nursemaid did not look in his direction again. Now he turned his head to the pillow. He would suck his thumb all evening.

Once a week, the stepmother took them to a doctor. Only, this doctor just wanted to talk. She was a thin, middle-aged woman with graying hair. The three of them sat in front of her, looking down at their shoes. When she could not get them to talk, she gave them paper and crayons. Draw me a picture, she told them. The girl drew pictures of women in kimonos. Is that your mother? the doctor asked. No, the girl said. I just like looking at women in kimonos.

The middle child drew pictures of airplanes and people falling down and cracking their heads on cliffs. The doctor would ask to speak to the father privately. This is very disturbing, the doctor said. She took the pictures and showed them to the boy's father. Your child is disturbed, she said.

The youngest drew nothing at all. If pushed, he would draw a square. Just an empty square, nothing else. Children like to draw, the doctor would tell him. He would shrug, let the crayon slip from between his fingers.

The girl's old piano teacher had moved away while they were in Manila. Now there was a new teacher: Russian, with steel-gray hair and wire-rimmed glasses. The girl found it difficult to understand her. Sometimes the teacher would become exasperated and after many times telling the girl to put her fingers on a particular key, she would reach out with her gnarled fingers, making the girl start and shrink backwards. The woman's fingers were hard from years of pounding the ivory keys. The girl was not interested in the piano. When her father heard her slow, hesitant practicing on the piano in the living room, it made him grit his teeth. He did not like to be reminded of his first wife, to whom the piano belonged. The piano had belonged to his first wife's mother for many years, and then she had it shipped to New York. His first wife loved to play Beethoven sonatas.

When Halloween came, the girl said she wanted to be Ginger Spice. She wanted a Ginger Spice jacket: short and tight, with a Union Jack motif. Then, when it came close to Halloween, she suddenly changed her mind and said she wanted to be Baby Spice, the pretty blonde one. She wanted the blonde pigtails and the short skirt and the spaghetti-strap top. To her surprise, the stepmother became very solicitous and immediately ordered up an outfit from a dressmaker, even taking the girl in for fittings after school. The middle boy said he wanted to be the stalker in *Scream*—the one who dresses in black and wears the mask. The father did not know anything about *Scream*, but there was a big toy store around the corner from their apartment. This toy store was on 87th street, and one weekend he took the boy there and they selected a costume that looked just like the one worn by the character in the movie: the white rubber mask with the trailing black hole for a mouth, and the black robe. The youngest child said he did not want to be anything. The stepmother lost her patience and called him "naughty." He spent a lot of time looking out the big plate-glass windows of their ninth-floor apartment, down at the street below. Whenever anyone asked what he was doing there, he would say he was counting yellow cabs.

Actually, he thought he had once seen the edge of his mother's cream bathrobe. The edge of it drifted out in the air, but she herself was around the corner of the building and he couldn't see her. "Come and see!" he'd cried out to his older sister, tugging her by the hand. When she'd come and looked, she said only, "That's the smoke from the roof of the next building." There was always some sort of smoke drifting by, from manholes on the street–something cooking down there, the boy would wonder?–or from the roofs of adjacent buildings. But the boy was sure that his mother was drifting outside the window. "She's come for me," he thought to himself. And afterwards, he was always by the window. The smoke that drifted by sometimes seemed to him to have a peculiar shape, like that of a woman peering in the windows. At these times he could not say exactly that it reminded him of his mother, but he was always watching and waiting for her.

Once he overheard an argument between his stepmother and his father. They were arguing about him, about why he liked staying by the window so much.

It's that woman, his stepmother was saying, and the boy knew she was talking about his old nanny. Came here the other day. Just dropped by, she said. Taking her new charge out for a stroll. He lives somewhere on 90th. They just happened to be passing by the building. She tells him things.

After that, the father said he would have a talk with the nanny. He would tell her she must not stop by anymore. It was bad for the children.

Early in the afternoon of Halloween, the aunt from San Francisco called. "Are you going trick-or-treating?" she wanted to know. "What are you going to be?" The two older children were very excited, describing their costumes to her. The youngest would not speak, and so the oldest girl said, "He's going to be a dog! He's going to follow me around on all fours, like a puppy!" This made the aunt laugh. She had no idea whether the girl was joking or serious. They told her that Regis Philbin, the talk show host, lived in their building, and that every Halloween he gave out huge parcels of candy. So they would be sure to ring the bell of his apartment. And there were a few other people in the building who gave a lot of candy, but most of the people were old women with harshly painted mouths and strings of pearls, who cared nothing for children holding out bags and asking for candy.

But the youngest child is distracted and doesn't think about Halloween. He sees his mother hovering outside the plate-glass window in a blue house dress decorated with tiny pink flowers. At least, he knows it is his mother, though her face is obscured by a shimmering whiteness. She stretches out her arms to him. He goes to the window, and he looks down, and her feet are standing on air. Now she stretches out both arms to him. Below him, the traffic on Park Avenue is snarled. A cab has tried to make a right turn from the wrong lane and now cars are beeping. But the noise is very far away. His mother is speaking to him. She says, over and over, "Not too good, not too good," and the child knows she is speaking about him. Because last night his stepmother spanked him. He had broken something, he can't now remember what. But it was in his stepmother's room, and it was precious to her. He knew it was precious only after it was broken. When the thing lay in shards on the carpet. Then his stepmother wailed. She called him a demon. She said there was something inside him, something bad, that made him do these things. His older brother and sister only looked on, frightened, when the stepmother was carrying on.

His father came. He was very angry and dragged the youngest child to his room. The youngest child stayed there all evening, sobbing.

One day, the youngest child was about to go out. He stood in the foyer, waiting for the elevator. Then he saw her, his old nanny. She seemed to have been waiting for some time. With her was a blonde child in a stroller. The youngest child looked in fascination at this other being, and remarked how its mouth seemed to form little O's at intervals, as though yearning to suck. The nanny hugged him to her. "You're so thin!" she kept saying, over and over. She brushed his hair out of his eyes. She asked after the other two children. "They're in their room, watching TV," said the youngest child. He was alone in the foyer with his old nanny, and it seemed his heart must burst from happiness.

They heard a noise. The woman gave a start. "I have to go," she said, trying to free her skirt from the youngest child's fingers. "No! No!" he cried. He buried his face between her legs. He thought he could smell damp earth there and he liked it. But she pushed him away. "If your father asks, you know what to say," she told him.

She hurried down the corridor to the elevator. Now the youngest child wandered to the window. Again he saw his mother there. Only now her face was distinct. He saw it clearly: the dark eyes, the full cheeks. Every feature of her face was as clear as a photograph. And she was looking at him with her arms outstretched.

He looked down at the avenue. The yellow cabs were there honking, but the sound seemed again to be coming from a great distance. The boy would have climbed on to the window ledge but his mother shook her head and mouthed the word "No." Her voice was gentle. He thought she looked sad.

Then the boy's sister came running out, looking for him. She saw him at the window and asked him what he was looking at. But the youngest child looked at his mother, and she had a finger raised to her lips, so he did not reply. Instead he pointed at the busy cabs on the avenue. The girl said, "You are a funny boy," and ran away again. The youngest child saw his mother looking longingly after her.

The youngest child saw his mother was wearing flowered cloth slippers. These he had seen in a box in the hall closet once. He went to the hall closet now. He rummaged among the boxes, but though he opened box after box, the one with the cloth slippers had disappeared.

One of the maids came out of the kitchen. "Bad boy!" she told him. "Look what a mess you've made! I will tell your father when he gets home!"

He looked again at his mother in the window. She only shook her head sadly at him and smiled.

Now the youngest child spent all his time at the window.

"What are you doing?" the stepmother said impatiently. "Get away from there!" She was afraid he might fall out. She knew of the terrible mishap of Eric Clapton's child. The maids were under strict orders to keep the boy away from the window.

But the maids were too busy to keep an eye on him all day. They were both from the Philippines and loved to talk to each other in the kitchen. There were long stretches of the day when they forgot about the youngest child. Left to himself, he always went to the window. His mother was always there now, waiting for him. She always brightened up when he came.

Once the boy tried to tell his sister what he was seeing. He asked his sister if she remembered her mother, and she said, "Of course!" He asked her what their mother had looked like, and his sister said, "She had black hair." He asked his sister if she would know their mother if their mother were to appear again. His sister gave him a strange look. "I would know her. Of course I would know her," she said. But no matter how often his sister passes the window, she never turns her head, even when her mother is staring straight at her. And this is how the youngest child knows he is the only one who can see his mother, his mother who waits by the window and looks in.

In November it began to snow. It snowed so hard that all the schools were closed for a few days. Then all the children were home, and the maids complained about how tired they were, picking up after them all day long. The stepmother was sick in bed with a cold. She never left her room.

The youngest child found that it was hard for him to see his mother sometimes, in the whirling snow. Her face was obscured by a strange whiteness. One evening, when his father was reading a newspaper in the living room, the youngest child saw his mother pass through the window glass–a white shape, more like mist than anything else–and come up to his father as he sat in his old armchair. She stood there for a few moments, and the youngest child held his breath. But his father merely scratched his nose and continued reading. Then his mother, who was now an indistinct white shape, began to make a slow

119

circuit of the room. She stopped before the piano. The lid was open and it seemed to the boy that the keys trembled, but they made no sound. Then she moved in front of a painting of his stepmother. It had been painted when the stepmother was only 19. She was very beautiful, with rich, flowing black hair and large, sparkling eyes. His mother seemed to shudder. At once her light refracted into many shimmering crystals. These hung in the air briefly and disappeared.

The middle child's nightmares grew worse. Once or twice the maids heard him call out "Cecilia" which was his dead mother's name. The maids whispered and crossed themselves. The stepmother became frantic. She said the apartment had been visited by evil spirits. One of her secretaries at work told her about exorcisms and she had her husband call a priest. The priest walked around the rooms, swinging a censer and intoning a blessing. The youngest child saw his mother watching from the window. She was smiling.

Then the stepmother insisted, We must sell the apartment. The hall was too short, she said. She wanted a better view. The father talked to a number of real estate agents. The children looked around them at the familiar rooms and did not know what to do.

The eldest collected her dolls and told them they would soon be going to a new place. She imagined that in the new place, the children's rooms would be as far away as possible from their father's room. "Then we'll hardly see him," she whispered to her favorite Barbie, the one who was dressed like Princess Jasmine in *Aladdin.*

The middle child took to lurking in the kitchen with the maids. They reminded him of his grandmother, with their strange talk, though the maids had lived in New York for so long that they remembered little about their home villages and would never go back there even if they could afford to. When the middle child slid on to a high stool and leaned his elbows on the kitchen counter, the maids only looked at him and laughed. They were not cruel, but the father was too busy; the stepmother too cold. They had heard of a grandmother in the Philippines, an aunt in San Francisco, but these relatives never came. The maids had the apartment to themselves most of the time. Their friends were envious because they had so much freedom. But the maids themselves were not happy. They grumbled that the master didn't pay them enough to stay in a haunted apartment, with three such unlikable children. So why pay attention to the boy? Let him sit there! They continued to chatter with each other.

The grandmother called again from the Philippines. It seemed to the children, listening from behind a closed door, that their father and their grandmother were having an argument. It seemed the grandmother didn't want the children to go to Mexico for Christmas. She seemed to be reminding their father of a promise of some sort. They heard their father say, "It's very hard. Don't press me; don't press me." This was followed by a long silence. When their father came out of the bedroom, he had his lips tightly pressed together.

And then one day the youngest child no longer saw his mother at the window. He stared and stared, but she was gone. The smoke was only smoke, drifting lazily by. He wondered if the old priest who had come and said the prayers, who had filled the rooms with the bad-smelling odor of incense, had anything to do with his mother's disappearance. He went again and again to the window. Yes, his mother was really gone.

He looked up at the gray sky between the tall buildings. He listened to the sound of traffic. He never again saw his mother's face, or watched her come through the glass as a white shadow.

The apartment on Park Avenue was sold after Christmas. Eventually the children grew up. The two oldest were sent to boarding school in England, as the father planned. England is a cold country, even in summer. The children never stopped dreaming about the Philippines, the warm beaches, the swaying palm trees. But they were only allowed to see their grandmother every other year. She had grown old and stooped. Her hands were gnarled, and it hurt her fingers to straighten them. It seemed to the children that each time they saw their grandmother, a gray circle around the pupils of her eyes had grown larger. A hump seemed to be growing out of the middle of her back. She walked with a cane. She still sighed and said, "If only your mother had lived, how proud she would be ..."

The girl went to college at Smith. She said she wanted to be a writer. The middle child drifted into college, though his grades were not quite as good as his sister's, and so he did not make it to an Ivy League school.

They were spoiled, the stepmother said. She was still beautiful, her hair still the rich black it had been when the children first met her.

The youngest child was killed in a car accident the year after the apartment on Park Avenue was sold. It was very strange. He was crossing the avenue to go home from school. People said there were no cars coming from either direction when he left the sidewalk. And he HAD looked, contrary to what a child of that age might have been expected to do. Suddenly a black jeep had appeared, seemingly out of nowhere. The boy was flung up in the air and landed on the jeep's hood. There was a sickening thud, and when he landed on the pavement, his head bloody, the bystanders saw his arms and legs were already purple and starting to swell up.

His old nanny came to the hospital to visit him. He was not conscious, but perhaps he felt her tears. They fell on his inert hands and sprinkled the white hospital sheet. She crossed herself over and over, and people who happened to be nearby said she was commending the boy's soul to his mother's care.

TVs

My mother wants me to send her a new TV. She says TVs in the Philippines cost over 25,000 pesos, almost $500. The one she wants is a 25-inch, either a Sony or a Mitsubishi.

When did my mother develop this craving for a new TV? When I was last home, in Manila, the TV in her bedroom seemed fine. The colors looked a little blurry, but it was the shows themselves I had a problem with. There was something called "TV Patrol", which reminded me of a grislier version of "Rescue 911". The last episode I watched, they were interviewing a father whose 11 children had just been murdered in a botched home invasion-style robbery. The father was crying, and there was a microphone being shoved almost up his nose.

There was also a children's show with singing Norwegians–at least, I think that's what the performers were supposed to be, because they had long, white-blond braids and Viking helmets. The variety shows featured hosts and hostesses with impossibly lacquered hair and sequined clothes against Day-glo bright, neon pink and green backdrops. I think: *There is nothing one can do, by buying a new TV ...*

My mother tells me we can ship the TV "door to door." Which is a way that Filipinos ship home boxes of Spam, corned beef, Vienna sausages and other coveted goods from America. There's no tax on the items, and the boxes aren't weighed. For a flat fee of $85, you can ship home anything that will fit in a standard-sized box. During the recent rice shortage in Manila, people even shipped home 50-lb. sacks of rice from the Price Club. Anything, as long as it fits in a 22-inch square box, can be sent home.

Now my mother brings up the name of my aunt and says:

"Tita Flor said you could send it to us for only $85."

I have been telling her the same thing for six months now,

but does she ever listen to me?

My mother is getting old. The last time I was home, I noticed she had stopped bothering to dye her hair. She looked strange: the ends of her hair were a shiny, artificial black, but the roots were all white.

I also noticed that she had stopped going to mass. Whether this had anything to do with my father's death the year before, I wasn't sure. My father was a diabetic, and before he died he'd developed gangrene and had to have some toes on his right foot amputated. All the relatives said, "It's only a matter of time," but my mother never believed them. Everyday she bathed my father's stump in saline water and examined it minutely for fresh cracks and fissures. My father eventually died of heart failure.

I went to visit his grave. It's not really a grave: just a niche in the wall, with his name in bronze letters, and the dates of his birth and death. I think my mother could pretty it up a little with flowers, but there was nothing there, on my last visit home. Only an empty vase, filled with stagnant green water. I emptied the water from the vase and filled it up again with some holy water from the font at the entrance to the funeral chapel. Then I walked around, surreptitiously snatching flowers from the grounds when the gardeners weren't looking.

When my mother said she wanted a new TV, I managed to avoid saying anything to my husband about it for three weeks. My husband is constantly talking about money–either that he needs to save more of it, or that I am spending too much. He says I never learned to save because my family is from Bacolod. Everyone knows that people from Bacolod are "big spenders". And my father was *splendido*–he spent freely, and he denied his children nothing.

I decide to call my husband at work.

"Mom wants a new TV," I say.

When he doesn't reply, I say, "Come on, her 60th birthday is coming up." My husband grunts and says he has to go.

When he gets home from work, he immediately switches on the TV. Of course. It's a Monday. There's a football game on. He buries his head in the paper.

One week, I'm in the Price Club, so I decide to check out the TVs. It's getting close to Thanksgiving. The place is colder than usual, and the Christmas things on display don't add to my cheer. The TVs are in a section by the entrance. They're lined up on shelves: all kinds of TVs, from the portable black-and-whites made in Korea, to huge monsters with stereophonic sound. People jostle and push, impatient at my meandering gait. A man in buckskin oxfords actually manages to tread on my toes. I calm myself by thinking: it will make my mother happy.

Which inevitably leads to thoughts of myself and my crummy job—I work as a secretary for a department at a private university, and my husband works in computer sales. We have just one child, a seven-year-old, but he's plenty for me to handle. When he comes home from school, spilling his tales of woe about classroom bullies, I sit down and tell him he comes from rich, rich stock in Manila.

My son only weighs about 50 lbs. He's small-boned, like my husband. And we've tried everything: giving him Enervon-C, which I ask the relatives to bring whenever they happen to pass by San Francisco; signing him up for karate lessons. His karate teacher yells and yells. During the sparring sessions, my son tries his best not to run away from his opponent, but never quite manages it. When he has his legs spread apart in what they call a horse stance, the karate teacher whacks at his feet with a pointer if they are not exactly parallel. The teacher tells my son to do crescent kicks. My son can hardly keep from falling down. Next year, I swear to God, I'll try injections. My mother says there's a doctor in Manila who'll do it. She says my brothers got injections when they were 11 or 12—there, it's no big deal. Of course, I need to keep this a secret from my son's American pediatrician. Dr. Eldon keeps telling me: "Well, look at your husband and yourself. You're only five feet, and your husband's maybe five foot five, so you can't expect apples to grow from orange trees, you know what I mean?"

Now, standing in the middle of Price Club, I am thinking: what the hell do I need to get my mother a new TV for? A couple of middle-aged women are standing behind tables at the ends of the aisles, holding out paper cups of food and yammering. One says, over and over in a monotone: "Delicious chicken-apple sausages, Aisle 11C, in the freezer to the right." She says this over and over without stopping, not caring if anyone is listening or not.

And I can't help asking myself: what is it that makes my mother the way she is? What makes Filipinos the way we are? Why can't a man who has lost his family nurse his grief in private? What is it that makes us beg for "door to door"? For new TVs? For Spam?

BLACK DOG

When I think of my childhood, I imagine a series of long afternoons spent in leafy gardens and sunny rooms. The air was golden, mottled with dust. Time stretched out: most of the time I read in my room, which had a balcony facing a creek; two beds: one for me and one for my older sister; and old chests filled with letters and greeting cards .

Our house always seemed to have a lot of people coming and going.

School was death. The hours dragged until I could come home and see my mother again, and taste the hot *guinataan* the cook prepared for my *merienda*. And always there would be something different to observe: another stranger's car parked in the driveway; a new vase of flowers on the antique chest by the front door.

One day I came home from school to find an old man sitting in the *sala* with my mother. I had never seen him before. He sat on one of our long wooden recliners, sipping a cup of hot chocolate my mother must have asked the cook to prepare especially for him.

He sipped slowly, carefully, and talked to my mother in *Ilonggo*, which was the dialect of the province to the south where my mother's family came from. I thought he might be a worker from one of my mother's farms. I went up to my room and did not think of the old man anymore.

Later, I heard my mother calling to me. "Come!" she said. "Do you want to go to the Polo Club?" So I knew the visitor had left. My mother spent every afternoon in the Club, playing bridge on a wide verandah that overlooked the polo fields. The other women who played there had lacquered hair and fingernails; silk dresses; perfume. Yes! I said. I loved to watch these women, so intent on what they were holding in their white hands, so languorous and free. Besides, the Polo Club had the best library, filled with American paperbacks.

While we were in the car on the way to the club, my mother sighed. I looked at her questioningly. She was shaking her head.

"A strange story," she said. She didn't speak for some minutes, while I tried to hold my tongue. Then, very slowly, she asked, "Do you know who that was?"

I shook my head, no. Such a question! It was part of a game my mother played, a kind of introduction to what I knew must be a wonderful story to follow.

"That was a friend of your *lola's*, your grandmother's. He'd just come from the farm. But he is really a justice. He comes from Aklan."

A justice! The man was old and stooped. He spoke in the native dialect. His clothes were worn.

My mother went on: "He told me the strangest story, about a case he had tried."

And she went on to tell me the story. The car wound slowly in and out of the leafy streets. And by the time we arrived at the Polo Club, I knew all about the case, a man tried for murder, and the black dog.

The story is really very simple: a man has a daughter who falls ill one day. He brings her to a doctor, a doctor who lives in the next *municipio*. It is almost a day's walk away, and the doctor prescribes this and that medicine, all of which costs a lot of money. The poor farmer spends his last savings on the medicine for his daughter, but her illness continues to advance. Finally, in desperation, the farmer consults a local *mangkukulam*.

Do you know what these people are, my mother asks me. "They are native healers. When people are cursed, as they so often are in the provinces outside Manila, usually by people who envy another's good fortune, the *mangkukulam* tells them how to get rid of the curse."

And suddenly I remembered seeing a dark man hovering over a pale woman lying naked from the waist up on a wooden table. Who was this woman? Where had I seen such a thing?

The man plunged his hands into the woman's chest and rooted around there. When his hands surfaced again, I saw they were bloody. Something white and shiny clung to his fingers. He flicked the matter into a wooden bowl that a servant had brought. The woman got up, holding a towel to her chest. It seemed she had been healed.

And another time, one of my aunts, who had a huge cataract in her right eye that had nearly blinded her, was sitting in our living room while a strange man pressed and pressed on her face until her eye seemed about to bulge out of its socket. The man had pulled out a green lump. "What is it?" my aunt had cried, holding her eye and crying. "*Muta*," the man said. Watching from under the table (I must have been only four or five years old), I had burst out laughing. Because the man had used the word for the repulsive crust that I sometimes found rimming my eyelids when I woke up in the morning.

My mother continued, "the *mangkukulam* told the farmer that his daughter was under a spell. And nothing could be done for her unless the farmer were to kill the thing that had put the spell on her."

"And what was this thing?" I ask.

My mother smiles indulgently at me. "The *mangkukulam* didn't know. It would show up at the farmer's house at midnight, that very night. Whatever it was, the farmer must kill it. This the *mangkukulam* emphasized, holding the farmer's arm in a tight grip, and looking straight into his eyes." My mother, at that point, also looked straight at me. If her hands had not been on the wheel, I felt sure she would have gripped my hands hard between her own. "You must not stop until the thing is dead," said the *mangkukulam*, who my mother described as being an old woman, unimaginably old, with matted gray hair.

How did my mother know all these details—how the *mangkukulam spoke*, what she looked like? Could Justice Makalintal have gone into such detail? Was my mother embellishing the story purely from her imagination? Or could one of those ancient women who I sometimes saw sitting on the *lanai*, having a cup of hot chocolate, could one of those possibly have been one of these creatures?

"And so," my mother told me, "the farmer went home, and he waited until midnight at the entrance to his hut. And, just after midnight, what should come along but a big black dog."

The dog was huge, it was enormous. Its eyes were red, its nostrils distended, and steam emanated from its flared nostrils. Its panting was so loud it drowned out all other sounds, including the beating of the farmer's heart. It sniffed around the house for a few moments, and then casually began to make a circuit around it. The farmer's heart contracted to see how familiar the dog seemed to be with the territory, and there was a terrible purposefulness to the animal's gait. The farmer could hear his daughter thrashing around on the bed inside the hut, and crying out as though beset by demons. Suddenly he could hear the sound of her body being dragged across the floor, as though by some superhuman force.

"But the farmer was patient. He waited."

"Why did he wait?" I asked.

"Why, because he trusted the *mangkukulam*," my mother says. And I know, though she does not say so, because it adds to the suspense, and because she so enjoys seeing my eyes grow rounder and rounder, there is never anything like this in the Literary Reader I have to slog through in Grade 6 at the Assumption Convent, the nuns at my school have no imagination and they are nothing, nothing like my mother.

"Finally, with a fierce yell"–the yell is to buck up his courage, my mother tells me–"the farmer attacks the dog with his *bolo*."

I have seen pictures of this curved, murderous-looking blade in the storybooks that tell how Lapu-Lapu decapitated that interloper Magellan. And the laborers on our farm use it to hack the stalks of sugar cane. Right and left they hack, their arms glistening with sweat. And, looking at their brown arms, tasting the juice of the sugar cane that they hand to me and my mother, I shiver, even under the noonday sun.

"The dog lets out a scream which sounds like no other,"

my mother says. "And suddenly, lying bleeding at the farmer's feet is a woman. A very beautiful woman, with long black hair. She kisses the farmer's feet. She begs for her life. The farmer is of course terribly surprised but he has no choice other than to hack at the woman until he is sure she is dead."

The next day, my mother tells me, the farmer is hauled off to jail and accused of murder.

"And is this how Justice Makalintal enters the story?" I ask.

My mother nods slowly. "Well, here is the courtroom and there in front of Justice Makalintal stands the accused. And how can Justice Makalintal make head or tail of this man's story. The man keeps insisting he is innocent, even though everyone has seen him with the bloody *bolo*, and there was a dead body at his feet when the policemen came to take him away. He told them about the *mangkukulam*, and so they had to send for her, and when she came the judge had to threaten her with jail before she would open her mouth. After hemming and hawing–a lot of that–she told the judge that yes, the farmer, was a client of hers, and yes indeed his daughter was very sick, but she had never told him to kill the woman. Oh, no! What he had to kill was the THING that came at midnight.

"Justice Makalintal scratched his head. For certain, there was a dead body. But no one in the town knew who the victim was, or who to believe.

"And the strangest thing," my mother said, "was that it turned out the woman was the *yaya*, the nanny, of a certain rich family in Manila. And she had asked the family for leave to visit her old mother in another island, which was not the island where she happened to meet her end. So no one knew what she had been doing in Aklan.

"A few people said they had seen the woman in the marketplace, a week before the farmer's daughter fell ill. Someone even said they saw the woman talking to the young girl, in a friendly way. Perhaps that was where the spell had been cast, in the middle of the marketplace, with all those people!"

"And what happened to the farmer then?" I wanted to know.

"Was he released?"

In truth, I never found out the ending to this story. I wanted my mother to tell me that the farmer was found innocent, but she was scornful of such niceties. She said only, "it is hard to say how justice works in small towns in the Philippines." And for many many years after, even when I was a grown woman and living in California, I thought of the farmer, the woman, the daughter, the black dog.

VISITS

In the summer, my mother wrote to say that she was coming. Little knots of fear came and went in my stomach.

My life was placid, like a river. But beneath the water were black stones, boulders full of secrets. When my mother came on one of her periodic visits from the Philippines, the waters parted somewhat, and if I looked down I saw their shapes. I did not like it when my mother visited.

The house smelled of new paint. It was described by the real estate agent who showed it to my husband and me last year as "California ranch type". My mind, in the days before my mother's coming, was like a sieve. Thoughts entered and left, leaving no trace.

In the mornings, the house was cold. A little bird made rapping sounds on the window in the kitchen. I thought it might be drunk from the berry bush that grew by the back door. The sound of the tapping wove through my day.

Now and then, I would think of Manila, all the people there. The cook in the kitchen; the *labandera* washing clothes at the outside sink; the driver lolling on the bench in the garage, waiting to be called. My mother in the garden; blurred figures in white uniforms, dusting the *santos* in the living room.

Here there was no one. No one. I would walk from the kitchen to the bedroom to the backyard. I would do laundry. I would water the plants. In that whole time, the phone never rang. After my husband left for work, there was no one to talk to.

———

In September my mother passed through San Francisco. She was on her way to New York to bring my sister's three children, who'd been on vacation in Manila, back to school.

Though my mother came to visit me at least once a year, it

was different this time. This time I didn't look forward to her coming, I don't know why. It seemed to me during this visit that my mother talked endlessly. Once she shocked me by carrying around the picture of my dead sister that I had framed and put on the mantelpiece. Then she looked at it for long moments, sometimes rubbing a forefinger over the dusty glass.

In the picture, which is black and white, my sister looks slender and charming. It was a way she sometimes used to look, though not often. In her last years, she was gaining weight and tended to look puffy. But in the picture she looks very nice. I have one just like it on my desk at work.

When the time came for my mother to go, I didn't ask her to extend her stay. I suppose I should have; I guessed this was what she might have been waiting to hear. And as the days dragged on and my mouth remained stopped up, my mother's face began to acquire a disappointed look. We said nothing to each other, however. When I took her to the airport, I didn't even park the car. Just dropped her off at the curb, gave her a quick hug, and hopped back on the freeway. I remember looking behind me once in the rear view mirror, but the view of my mother was obscured by other people and moving vehicles.

Then I heard from time to time about her doings in New York. Sometimes I called. Once I called on a Sunday afternoon. It must have been early evening in New York. I could hear the voices of my sister's children in the background. Arguing about something. I imagined the twilight creeping down the avenues, the muffled noise of traffic. She said, "Oh, where were you, where were you?" She'd been trying to reach me all afternoon, she said.

"I was at the office," I said. "I have so much work."

"Oh," she said. "I called and called, but no one answered the phone."

"Why? What's wrong?" I said.

"Well," she said. "They went to the park, and I said it's better that *sila na lang*, you know what I mean, three is a crowd, I didn't want to be *asungot*."

134

"What are you talking about?" I asked. "Who is 'they'?"

"Oh, you know," my mother said. "Harry and Rita. Oh, but it hurts. It hurts."

Rita is my brother-in-law's new girlfriend. She manages an art gallery in mid-town Manhattan. She and my brother-in-law had been seriously dating only a few weeks, just since August. Rita has black hair and a deep golden tan. She looks nothing like my sister.

I imagined my mother alone in the apartment, surrounded by my dead sister's things. I wondered if my sister's needlework was still in the drawer next to her bed. Soon, I thought, my mother will start having to put her things away. I thought of my sister's pretty silk dresses hanging in the closet, her shoes lined up neatly on the wooden shoe racks. While some of her shoes were very badly scuffed, others seemed barely worn. I remembered my mother telling me how once, borrowing one of my sister's coats, she'd reached into the pockets and found an old tube of lipstick, worn down almost to the stump, and wads of used Kleenex. This of course made my mother cry. I remembered my reaction when my younger brother wanted to cash a Traveler's Check with my sister's signature on it. "No, no!" I cried. "Here's a hundred dollars of my own. "Take it, take it!" I was beside myself.

Once, when I was visiting my brother-in-law, we wound up talking about my sister's shoes, I don't know why. Perhaps it was my first visit to the apartment after her death, and my first look at her closet. It was strange that I had never actually seen the inside of her bedroom when she was alive.

I had been amazed by the sheer quantity of her things, and especially by the neatly arrayed rows of shoes, rising along one wall from floor to ceiling. "Yes," my brother-in-law said to me, "she hardly even used most of them, poor thing."

And it was actually hard for me to think of my sister in that way–as a "poor thing." Because she had never been what the nuns at our convent school might have called "good." In fact, she was rather mean. Even when we were teenagers, I can read in my old diaries about times she dragged me off my bed and kicked me or pulled my hair. But thinking of these episodes now does not fill me with bitterness. On the contrary, I am glad I have such memories, because I can say to myself that at one time I did have a sister.

It isn't true, what a friend once said. She was visiting from Manila and we were talking, and the talk suddenly turned toward my sister. We were in the kitchen, and suddenly my friend said in a vehement way, "A sister like that–who pulled your hair and dragged you off the bed–is that what you miss?" At first I thought: She's right. I thought no more of my sister for a few weeks. But now I think she wasn't right at all. Because in fact it is those hard slaps my sister used to deliver to my face, my arms, that makes me remember her and brings tears to my eyes. Those hard slaps and scratches–one scar still visible on the back of my left hand, after all these years.

It isn't sentimental. I don't like to sentimentalize. It isn't the same thing as my mother walking around with my sister's picture all day. It's just remembering her the way she was. She slapped me, so that's all there is to it. She also pulled my hair and, during one of Manila's periodic blackouts, used to pretend she was a witch and cackle and put strong hands around my throat until I screamed. All those things she did.

And in fact, in a perverse way, I do remember her more because of those bad things. Those things I thought were purely evil. Like the time she slammed the closet door over my fingers as she saw me reaching to open the top drawer. I must have been–what?–five years old and she six. Already in her mind that obscure hatred of that Other, that Other of flesh so dissimilar from her own. Because while I was bouncing and jolly and plump and easily given to smiles and laughter, my sister was a skinny little thing, with hard knees always covered with scrapes and bruises, and a small mouth my mother had to pry open with a spoon sometimes to get her to eat her vegetables. Once I'd come home from somewhere and seen my best doll, the one with the cornflower blue eyes and the curly brown hair, thrust upside down into the toilet. I howled then as if someone had actually killed me, as if a knife had actually been plunged right into my chest. There, there, there. But it was only my sister. Only the pain and confusion over having such a sister.

Now, I tell myself, it isn't wrong to slip on her pantyhose or to wear her shoes. They were the first things my mother brought over from New York. I didn't question my mother then, though I'm sure I could have. I do not question her now.

The pantyhose was sheer and fragile-looking, mostly in shades of gray and blue. At first I kept them tucked away in a corner of my closet. Out of sight.

The shoes we spread out in the garage. They were in all colors: blue, green, black, red. Some were misshapen, and reminded me of my sister's feet, with their bunions and their plump toes.

The first ones I wore were brown, with straps and pointy toes. I looked in the mirror at myself wearing them. My legs suddenly looked long and very slim. "I like these," I said aloud. My mother didn't seem to take any notice.

The other shoes she gave away–to my cousin Ana, to an elderly lady who had just lost her secretarial job at an accounting firm. I did not like to think of my mother giving my sister's things away, but she never asked me. I saw my aunt and my cousin leaving the house, their arms bulging with paper bags.

My sister had a black sweater with a green rosette pattern. That one I wore to a dinner one weekend, and everyone exclaimed at how good I looked, how "young." I felt like telling them, "This is my sister's sweater. She's dead, you know. She died a couple of years back." But I thought it would be too strange. No one I know says things like that. Though saying things about my sister makes me feel good, perhaps because I did it so rarely when she was alive.

Now there are times when I find myself telling perfect strangers: "My sister died last year. Streptococcal pneumonia. It was quite a shock." Sometimes the stranger will frown and say nothing. Other times he or she will shake their heads and look concerned. Most often, they will look solicitous and say, "I'm sorry!" It's the ones who look silently mournful that I despise. Because I know it's a pretense. How could someone else possibly understand what it is like? "There, there," I feel tempted to say. "It's not your fault. I'll survive."

During my aunt's visit, she complained that I keep too many lights on in the house. She said that in Manila, everyone is trained to turn the lights off whenever they leave the room. But then, she said, "I know why you do it. It's on account of the little boy." She referred, I suppose, to Johnmel, who is seven years old now, and not particularly afraid of anything, not even of the dark.

I remain silent, knowing I cannot answer her, wishing to preserve some peace. But in bed at night, strange thoughts creep into my head, and one time I imagine myself saying to someone, not necessarily my aunt, "Someday, someday all the lights will be off, and then I'll be dead."

BMW

One summer, my father came to San Francisco for an operation on his foot.

Over the years, he'd lost parts of his limbs to diabetes. Now what worried my mother was his right foot, where he'd already lost the big toe. There was a fresh cut that refused to heal, even after my mother diligently poured saline solution over it and covered it with fresh bandages each morning and night.

When he came to stay with us in San Francisco, parts of the foot were already completely black. I marveled at my mother's nonchalance. "Perhaps," she said, "the doctor will only need to cut away a little of the flesh."

A little of the flesh? My dreams were filled with the sight of my father's blackened foot on my mother's lap. When she first removed the bandages and revealed the foot to me, I had to press my fist tight against my mouth to stop from crying out. Yet, my mother said, "This is nothing. The doctor will take care of it."

But it turned out the doctor would not be available for a month. And it seemed to me that the foot was getting blacker. Unbeknownst to my mother, I would call the doctor's office and plead with the nurse. "Please," I would say. "This is an emergency. You should see his foot. My mother doesn't realize ... its almost completely black. But because my father doesn't complain, my mother thinks it's all right. He doesn't feel any pain; he's diabetic. His nerve endings may have been damaged."

The doctor finally agrees to see my father and, yes, they have to amputate. This news almost destroys my mother.

In the hospital in San Francisco, nightmare upon nightmare: they happen to give my father a faulty bed, one with a side guard that will not rise. My mother points this out to one of the nurses and the nurse assures her they will take care of it. But in the middle of the night, the day of my father's operation, he rolls off because the side guard is down. He lands on the floor with a thud and then lies there, stunned. The noise awakens his roommate, a Mr. Schmidt who is retired and lives somewhere in Marin County. He and my father have gotten along famously since the moment they met. Mr. Schmidt leans over and asks my father, "Are you all right? Shall I call a nurse?"

And my father says yes, I am all right, and who knows by what test of will manages to pull himself up and back on to the bed.

The next morning, he says nothing to the nurses. He waits until my mother arrives and then tells her. My mother is angry, but in talking to the nurses finds no relief. The nurses are defensive. They begin to criticize her for talking to my father in Tagalog in front of them. My mother is upset, she is always upset. My parents go home. We thought it was behind us. The hospital agreed to bill my parents on an installment basis. They did not have insurance: the bill reached almost $20,000.

My father sent the payments to me, along with the payment stubs, for me to send to the hospital. He was a very conscientious man and never talked about the hospital bed or his accident, though my mother talked about it constantly and railed against the hospital. I had just made the fourth payment when I received the news that he had died.

It was very quick: having breakfast with my mother one morning, he'd felt unwell and gone up to his room. He'd only been up there a few minutes when the intercom buzzed loudly once, twice. The cook's teenage daughter, Juliet, answered it. She ran to get my mother in the garden. Everyone ran up the stairs together: the cook, the daughter, my mother. When they reached the bedroom, my father was already slumped over, his eyes open. My mother called the driver and together they tried to revive him. But, as my mother said to me later, over the phone, "No more *na.*" My father was dead.

I had a letter started the previous September, in my drawer. "Dearest Dad," it began, and then, the blank page. My father died in February.

My father's death was not tragic or shocking. Although he was only 63 years old, we didn't expect him to live very long. We had eyes. We could see how stiffly he moved down the corridor, groping along the walls for support. How his legs looked, stick-thin and pale, the color of fish bellies, as his robe dangled open.

Whenever I think of him, the phrase "like a Buddha" comes to mind, because of my father's girth, his inscrutable features, never marred by emotion of any kind, whether pleasure or anger.

———————

Last year I received a letter from Mr. Schmidt. The letter said, "How are you? How is your father? I hope he will get in touch the next time he is in San Francisco."

I kept the letter in my handbag for weeks, waiting for the right time. Then, one afternoon, when it was bright and sunny out, when my son was at school, I took out pen and paper and wrote:

"Dear Mr. Schmidt, my father died four months after the amputation of his foot. He died in Manila. His death was quick and painless and I am sure he did not suffer. My mother is a strong woman. She busies herself with charity work, in Manila and elsewhere. I wish you all the best. I hope you are recovering nicely."

For weeks after posting the letter, I kept expecting to hear from Mr. Schmidt. I remembered him well: a nice man, who reminded me a little of that fatherly actor on "Saint Elsewhere." But there was no more news from him.

Later, my husband told me, "It must have been a shock, your writing to him that your father died." And, yes, I think now that it must have been. And I regret the letter, and its tone. What kind of tone was that? How does one really know how to write about death?

When my father was alive, I brought home a BMW. Yes, I actually shipped one home, registered in my name. It was the one time in my life I brought home anything my parents wanted. I had just graduated from an all-girls' college in California. I hadn't been home in three years.

We ran into problems picking it up from the pier. It turned out some congressman had his eye on it. We had to hire an "expediter"–a person referred to us by a man married to one of my cousins. We were sure the man married to my cousin knew everything there was to know about such things because he had once found a way to ship home guns from California in tins. I remember visiting him in Redwood City, where he was staying with a friend, and watching him seal the tins at the kitchen table.

The "expediter" turned out to be a woman who operated out of a tiny office in a slum near the port area. We drove there, my father and I, in his creaky old Mercedes. Everyone pointed at us and laughed. We were driving around and around these narrow, twisting streets. The houses looked as though they might fall down at any moment. The lady came out of the backroom. My God, her stomach was enormous. How did she ever get into this business? She must have been six, seven months along. Later she disappeared into the back room and I heard a string of filthy language–*Putangina mo, Puñeta, Coño,* Asshole, Shit! It could only have come from her, though when she reappeared she seemed remarkably composed and said to my father only, "Hmm, yes, where were we?"

Then she told my father, "Well, if you want your car, that will be $4,000." $2,500, she explained, was for the payoffs, and $1,500 was her standard fee. My father was very relieved and paid her the money right on the spot. And the next week he had his car.

When my father died, the BMW was sold, rather cheaply, to a Chinese businessman who owned a string of hardware stores around Manila. There had been problems with the car for some time. My father had only used it occasionally, after all.

WANTING

Everyone said, "Teresa is so sensitive." She imagined slights and hurts where none were intended and spent hours in a storm of crying up in her room. Even her inability to have another child, she attributed to her doctor's dislike.

A long time ago, Teresa wanted to have a child. This was–oh, so many years ago, when she was 30. She remembered lying on her back on the cold table in the doctor's office, looking at the black and white screen of the ultrasound scan. The screen showed the doctor the size of her ovaries, inflamed just then by Clomid.

"There, there, there!" the doctor exclaimed, looking with something almost like love at the largest polyps, blooming like strange coral flowers on the screen.

Hope rose in her at such moments.

She lived in San Francisco. She had one child already, a girl. This girl meant everything to her. She meant even more to Teresa than her husband did, who came home every night promptly at six and supported them all without a murmur of complaint.

When she used to bring her daughter home with her to Manila for a visit, people would say, "Carissa is the love of your life." Their saying this used to make her feel happy.

She remembered when her daughter was a shape growing in her belly. She remembered how, with every passing month, this shape grew and grew, until it became alive beneath her fingers, so that she could distinguish the tiny imprint of a foot, a hand, on her stomach, when it was near her time to deliver. Her husband never did such things as press his ear to her rounded belly, to hear the baby's heartbeat. He rarely touched her at all, those days. But she knew when he looked at her that what she felt was love. It enveloped her, very much the way the baby inside her was embraced by the warm fluid of its amniotic sac.

She liked to think those were magical days, but perhaps she was exaggerating. They lived in a tiny apartment. They were foreign students at a university. They weren't writing to her husband's parents because the parents would keep asking them for money, perhaps not realizing that graduate students were poor.

And yet, she had to ask herself, how could grown people in their fifties not know this? And then she realized, they were blinded by America, by the idea of it: the immensity of the prospect of her husband graduating with an engineering degree and actually earning in dollars. Dollars multiplied 45, 50, even 60 times, in pesos. A hundred dollars could get many, many things in Manila, at that time.

Each time the letters came, always in the same long envelopes with the border of red and blue trim, she felt her breath constrict. She hardly knew what she was doing: she'd find herself outside the apartment building, in her nightgown. She'd forget to watch for traffic at street corners, and find herself dodging cars. People yelled at her a lot. She felt small– small like nothing. That was the effect those letters had on her.

They didn't know, at the time, what was going to happen to them. Whether they were going to be able to stay and find jobs in America after graduate school, or have to go back home. They never spoke about it to each other. It was the unspoken, unnameable Terror that even to mention would have been like mentioning The Evil Eye.

Sometimes she still walks by that apartment building where they used to live. It seems a cheerful place: vines cover the walls; trees grow in the front yard. She tries and imagines the people who lived with them at that time, their neighbors. Across the way was an 86-year-old woman named Estelle who died when Teresa was in her fifth month of pregnancy. One day, when they were at class, an ambulance came and when they arrived home that evening they heard from one of the neighbors that Estelle was in the hospital. She never came back, and her apartment stayed empty for a long time.

Sometimes she looked over at the blank window. She remembered how Estelle told her once that she liked looking across at their place, because of a lamp that they had set on their dining room table. It was a clear glass lamp from Macy's, a present from her mother.

"How cheerful it looks," Estelle said. "I like looking at it."

In the unit above Estelle lived the Mercereaus, an old couple, childless, in their nineties. She always felt their childlessness marked them in some way. When she thought of them, it was always with this implicit question in the back of her mind, a question that began to take the form of a criticism: Why couldn't they have children? Why? Why?

Instead, they had become like each other's children, always exclaiming over this or that ailment suffered by the other, always scolding each other if one of them forgot to wear a jacket in a cold wind. When she saw one or the other of them coming down the street, she always tried to avoid them. When she was pregnant, she would even try, ineffectually, to shield her growing belly from them. She didn't like it when they looked at her with their pale, watery eyes. The sadness that came from them was like a reproach.

Time moved with strange rapidity, the last months of her pregnancy, and almost before she knew it, the baby arrived. It was July. Her water broke, when she was alone in the apartment. She sat on the toilet seat, looking dully at the stains on her underwear, puzzling over the strange bits of matter, the consistency of cottage cheese, that came out with the water, wondering what on earth they were. She decided to call the hospital, and the doctor said to come in right away.

"But I'm not in labor," she said.

"We still have to check you," he said.

Another neighbor drove her to the hospital. They called her husband at his department in the university, and he came right away.

When he arrived, she was sitting in a birthing room, hooked up to a monitor that emitted regular, faint beeps. The heavy

147

black strap around her belly felt strange. They were inducing her with Pitocin.

Seventeen hours later, Carissa was born. She heard a thin cry, there was a sudden warm weight on her chest. Looking down she saw two black eyes gazing solemnly at her. Then this shape was scooped up in a blanket by a nurse, and she was being wheeled into the recovery room.

Four years later, when they started trying to have another baby, they found they couldn't. They were both still in America; they both had jobs. This time, their lives were more settled.

Because, in spite of all their fears, they had achieved their dreams, they'd attracted the Bad Luck that was to follow them all the rest of their married days.

Because they hadn't gone home.

The letters in the long envelopes with the blue and red trim continued to come from his parents, saying why, why, why?

They moved to another place, to a townhouse of their own, in a new development built on landfill by the bay. The ground was dry and rocky. Small, stunted trees grew in concrete planters on the sidewalks. In the daytime, the subdivision was completely empty and had the feeling of a ghost village. Teresa stayed home in the afternoons and waited for the first sounds of the arriving cars, sometime around 5:00. Then she liked to listen to the squeal of brakes on driveways, the sounds of automatic garage doors opening, one after the other.

Carissa (she'd referred to her daughter as "it" until Carissa was almost a year old, as though fearful to form too powerful an attachment to something that might be lost at any moment,

148

snatched away by some terrible calamity) grew into a strong and sturdy girl. Quite playful, in contrast to her solemn mother and father. At birth she'd been almost 8 and a half pounds.

"It's what happens when you foreign mothers get that good American milk," the doctor had told her.

She was five foot one. At Carissa's birth, the doctor had written in her chart, "cephalopelvic disproportion." This was what had accounted for the 17-hour labor.

As a baby, she'd woken five, six times a night until Teresa thought she would go mad with exhaustion. Her husband sometimes slept with Carissa in her room; he was kind to her, in those days. It was only later that he began to develop that angry look, that look that seared her to the bone.

There was an unexpected downturn in the economy and her husband lost his job. They went from one lawyer to another, asking, do we have to go home? His previous company had been claiming him for a green card. With only one more year to go before the interview, they cut him off.

They had to bring the baby with them, while they were seeing the lawyers. Her husband went alone into the lawyer's office, and she waited outside, jiggling the baby carriage to keep the baby entertained. Sometimes she'd say "Hoo, Haa!" and make big round eyes at the baby, between her fingers. People stared. They didn't know that she had a masters degree in business administration. They thought she was a weird young woman who was perhaps faintly addled, making ridiculous sounds to a rather passive baby that was lying in a carriage and looking up at her with expressionless black eyes.

One lawyer said he would charge them only $500 to "research" the question of whether they could stay in America or not. Because he happened to be a Filipino, and because his office impressed them by being in a prestigious address in the business district near the Embarcadero, they paid him on the spot. And they never heard from him again. Not even when they made repeated phone calls to his office, and took to writing him letters. Finally, six months later, an exasperated secretary called the lawyer to the phone.

"I have researched the question," he said.

"And–?" Teresa said, impatiently.

"Yes, it appears you can stay," he said.

And that was all. He hung up, and she knew they had been fooled.

Such a rage came over her then. But there was nothing, absolutely nothing, she could do to get their money back.

After many weary months, there was an upswing in the fortunes of the Valley. They heard her husband's old company was re-hiring, and even though it was humiliating for him, he went back to his old boss, begging. And he was re-hired. So the next year, all three of them, with the baby, went to the Immigration Office on Sansome Street for their green card interview. They left their townhouse early, on a raw day in January, before it was even light outside. Their interview notice said 8 AM, but they had to wait for hours in a crowded waiting room. Finally, their number was called. They were interviewed separately, which meant that one of them could stay outside and watch the baby.

At her interview, the blonde young man sitting across the desk asked her how many American presidents had been assassinated. She responded quickly, two.

"And their names?" he asked, his face smooth as paper.

"Well, Lincoln, and Kennedy," she said.

"There were actually three," he responded. And rattled off a third name, so quickly she couldn't quite catch it. But it wasn't a name she would have recognized, in any case.

Then he made some cryptic marks on a sheet of ruled yellow paper, and asked her how many justices sat on the Supreme Court. Nine, she said, and he nodded, as though encouraging her.

"And their names?" he said.

She looked blankly at him.

"I—I," she began, before falling completely silent.

A stillness hung in the room. The young man looked at her, then rattled off nine names very quickly. She nodded, defeated.

Now, she thought, he'll kick me out and say you're a stupid woman who doesn't deserve to be granted permanent residency.

But when he stood, he shook her hand and said, Congratulations. She wandered out to her husband, and her air was so distracted that he became alarmed.

"What is it? What is it?" he asked her over and over, taking her arm.

"Nothing," she said. "It was nothing. I think I passed my interview."

But her face was very pale.

Their green cards came in the mail six months later. By this time, the tone of the letters from Manila had changed—had become increasingly strident, angry. Her own sudden access to good fortune only increased her guilt. She thought of lying to her husband's parents, saying they'd been denied green cards. But how then to explain why they were still not coming home?

We have no food, her mother-in-law wrote. *We are reduced to recycling nails. I have not bought myself a new dress in five years.*

They sent his mother a check for a hundred dollars for her birthday. This only seemed to arouse the woman to a fury.

Thank you for your check, she wrote back, in a letter dripping with sarcasm. It might pay for groceries for a week or so.

Prices had gone up so much, his mother explained. It was truly astronomical, the cost of food these days. They would be reduced to scrounging in the garbage. Or perhaps selling their car, which was their only means of transportation, now that they were too old to walk to the commercial district.

And that was when they decided to start trying to have another child. This time, it wasn't the powerful coming together that had characterized their making of Carissa. This time, a pall of uncertainty hung over all their actions, so that even when they were in bed together their motions were tentative, ill-defined, and no matter what they did she could not come and the milky semen spurted out between her legs almost as soon as it went in.

After a year, when she was still not pregnant, they decided to see a doctor. The doctor said he would do a diagnostic laparoscopy.

"But we will not call it infertility," he explained. "For insurance purposes, we will call it endometriosis."

And that was the first time she heard the dread word, a word she didn't even know the meaning of at the time, but which she later knew to associate with strange growths, masses, tentacles spreading inside her uterine cavity. That was the first time she knew also the name for the pain that attacked her on either side of her navel, every month, two weeks after her last menstruation.

This pain, however, was nothing compared to the pain of seeing her husband turn his face away from her whenever she spoke, as though the very sound of her voice hurt him.

After this, their monthly coming together was a scheduled thing, a routine act they performed when the doctor told them the timing was propitious.

––––––––

Many years later, she has come to look back on this time with just a hint of sadness. Just a slight trace of melancholy around her eyes. People who don't know will say of her, what a lucky woman, she has had nothing but brilliant opportunities, all throughout her life. And look at her now, living in that big house in Hillsborough, with the daughter who is doing so well at Stanford, and the gardener and the cook and the housemaids. There will be women who meet her at luncheons who will say, "How well she looks! How young!"

She hides her hurt well, but it is always there, just beneath the surface–when she hears about someone's pregnancy, or when she happens to glance at her husband, lost in thought as usual in front of the television.

There is nothing, nothing in the world she would not give to have that moment back, that moment in time when her husband and she are sitting across from each other at the dining table in their first little apartment, both silent with fears that are too terrible to name.

The Evil Eye will find you, wherever you are.

BAD THING

It was October. Dela was driving along when suddenly she felt sick, as though she anticipated hitting a car or a road barrier. She could see the collision in her mind, almost hear the thud of something hitting her bumper.

Her son turned six that year. She realized that, for weeks, she had been expecting something to happen. Driving him to school, a feeling would come over her and she would slow down and look furtively right and left, right and left. When they arrived at the school without mishap, she would be surprised and thankful, though she didn't know who she should be thankful to, she wasn't the praying sort. Dela would ease her unsteady legs out of the car, call to her son with some measure of confidence, and push herself through the rest of the day. Like that.

Finally, on the 17th of November, after months and months of her expecting something to happen, the man on a bicycle crashed into the front passenger side of her shiny red Corolla, and scraped both his forearms. Her son was not with her this time, thankfully. She was in unfamiliar surroundings, in Berkeley, where everything was a lot dirtier than down where she worked, at Stanford; where paper wrappers blew around in the street; where the students sat on the sidewalks on Telegraph Avenue as though completely unconcerned about germs and hygiene; where people bumped into her as she wandered around on the sidewalk asking directions, causing her to remember her purse.

She heard the thud before she turned and saw him. When she turned, she saw a man's face, grimacing, pressed against the window. She was out of the car immediately, and grabbed the handlebars of his bike. *Are you all right? All right? I'm so sorry.*

How stupid! She'd never even seen him. He'd been biking on the sidewalk. She'd been aiming for the entrance of a parking garage, but had been momentarily distracted by

155

a sign that said: Sorry, Lot is Temporarily Full. And, staring at this sign in disbelief–disbelief because it was still so early in the morning—she'd found herself asking: What sort of crazy place is this?

Earlier, she thought she'd found a parking place, in a two-level garage on another street. But, just to be sure, because nothing about this place made her feel sure, she asked a couple of students if you had to pay to park there, and they said yes, and when she asked where they said you had to get a little ticket from a metal dispenser up by the entrance. And walking to the entrance, she suddenly saw a big sign that she'd not seen earlier. It said: This Lot is Reserved Parking for Students Only, M-F, 7 AM-5 PM. And it was 10 AM, so she could not park there. Thank goodness she had thought to ask the students! The sign warned that "Violators Will Be Towed Away." And she didn't want that to happen, not in her current state anyway, not with her feeling as though any unexpected occurrence would find her chipping and cracking, like the paint on an old wooden doll.

She was standing on the sidewalk, all five foot two inches of her, and the young man, who was very tall, who was at least six feet, and who had the pale, pinched look of an ascetic, was still bent over, inhaling deeply, though he refused all her offers: *Shall I take you to a clinic? No? But your arm, look at your arm.* Just in the few short moments they'd been standing there, she could already discern black and blue around the edges of the scrape, a telltale swelling. And another spot, on his hand, that was red and raw.

Dela grasped the handlebars. *Let me fix your bike. Let me take you to work. We can put the bike in the trunk of my car, and I'll drive you.* But the young man, whose name, she found out later, was Henrik, said simply: *Just watch out for bikers next time, OK?* Yes, yes, oh yes! But how could she tell him—she'd known this would happen for months, but she hadn't known when or how. And then she had a new thought: what if she were to go forward now, forgetting about that old feeling, thinking the bad thing she felt sure was about to happen had happened, and suddenly, something even worse, the real Bad Thing, came along?

She thought back to the hospital and what happened to her brother. All the years they were growing up, and even up to the time they were married and starting their families, and had both moved to America, her brother was the Bad Thing. Anything her brother did made her ill. Her brother got a promotion at work. Oh, how happy it made Dela's mother to tell her. Her brother got a million dollar bonus for Christmas. Their mother told all the relatives.

But she, Dela, would lock herself in the garage, smoking furiously. After a while, people noticed. Where is Dela? What is she doing in the garage? Come out of there! What do you think you are doing–?

Maybe some of this feeling finally communicated itself to her brother, because in the last year, the year before his death, he had not called. No, not even to let Dela know that his wife was pregnant with their third child. Dela found out from their mother, a month before the baby was due.

And then, six months after the baby was born, six months after Miguel, her brother died. Since he had been young and seemingly healthy, only 36 years old, there had been an autopsy. The autopsy report stated "viral pneumonia." He had caught the flu, and it just dragged on and on, and like any typical thirty-six-year-old man, he'd continued to go to work, in the big bank in Manhattan, and he had continued to go out for dinner with his wife and his friends. Those who saw him at this time remembered a hacking cough, nothing more. And then, a few days later, he died. Just like that. No one could explain it.

And Dela had thought her brother was the Bad Thing! Her brother's death was even worse! Now she saw her brother everywhere!

A few months before her brother had died, she had gone home to the Philippines for a visit. Their mother had owned farms in Cebu, an island south of Manila. There, an aunt had told her a fascinating story. Her aunt's only daughter, a girl of 16, had suffered a terrible disfigurement. A black mark had appeared without explanation on her cheek, and as the days progressed this black mark grew and grew, to the point where it nearly eclipsed her entire face. No doctor could determine the cause, but her aunt had taken the girl to a *mangkukulam*, a medicine woman. And this woman had cured her of the bewitchment.

Dela had wanted to meet this woman, and so her aunt arranged it. The *mangkukulam* lived in a *nipa* hut down a narrow alleyway. The woman told Dela, "You have a twin. Your twin is of the spirit world. It follows you wherever you go. Turn your head quickly and you might see it, at the corner of your eye." Dela turned and turned her head; she never saw the merest shadow.

The old woman had given Dela an ointment to rub on her belly. For facilitating–what? *Gamot sa nerbiyos*, the old woman had said. For curing nerves. Funny, Dela had taken the ointment with her to the hospital in New York, those last few days before her brother passed away. What could she have been thinking? Was she going to rub it on her brother's belly–her brother, who may occasionally have been lost or even confused but had never in his life—so far as she knew—ever been frightened or nervous? Even at the hospital, with a respirator in his mouth, he had tried to crack a smile at her. Stupid woman, she berated herself–you've gone daft, finally. She hid the ointment in her bag and told no one. Though later, looking at her brother in the hospital bed, looking at how bloated he'd become, she was tempted to lift the edge of his hospital gown and rub the ointment on his stomach. Just in case. Just to try anything. Because nothing the doctors did seemed to help–not the antibiotics, not the hydrocortisone, not the ventilator, not the Pavulon, so perhaps this? This ointment from an old woman in Bacolod, from the other side of the world.

Hadn't the old woman decorated her one-room nipa hut with images of the Santo Niño and the Sacred Heart of Jesus? All those bleeding crucifixes and stigmata and curly-headed white saints. The bottle was filled with a sweet-smelling clear liquid and stalks of what looked like, must be, seaweed, and something else–a long sliver of hard white bone that she'd once crazily imagined had come from someone's finger. Hadn't the old woman breathed three times on the vial and clenched Dela's hands tightly between her own and said the ointment was good, good, good?

She did not administer the ointment to her brother. Perhaps that was why, later in the week, her brother died. Her brother died, and not even with anyone around him that he knew. He passed away in the elevator, while they were bringing him up to the operating room for a tracheotomy. Dela could imagine the scene in the elevator–the panic, the pandemonium. Could they get a heart machine in there? Were they giving him EKG shocks right in there? Later, when they were all at the hospital, her brother was already in a winding sheet, his hands–poor hands! Still with traces of ink stains from the last report he'd been writing–already tied together.

Dela returned to California, to her husband and son. Her mother, who had remained in New York, called her from time to time. She told Dela over and over about how the sight of her brother's tied hands made her unaccountably angry. The bruises on her dead brother's wrists and ankles were reminders of the times they had to strap him down to the bed because he was thrashing around, like a drowning person. Oxygen starvation, was what they told their mother. Ah, the terror of drowning and of being tied down! Tears would come to Dela's eyes at the thought.

So this Bad Thing, her brother, was not really the Bad Thing she had thought it was. The real Bad Thing was the hospital, the indifferent nurses and doctors, the endless probing of her brother's helpless body, and, finally, the lonely death in an elevator. Dela would never forget that lesson.

––––––––––––

She couldn't get the man out of her mind. Henrik. She saw him approaching the car, and suddenly her angle of perception would shift and she was   him, riding blithely along on a fine red bike, on a fine morning that was warmer than you'd expect in November, and she suddenly saw herself in her red Corolla, flashing out of nowhere, and she knew without a doubt that the whole thing was her fault. Never mind what she told her husband later: that the man was obviously biking too fast, that he wasn't looking or he would have seen her, that he should have stopped before crossing the entrance to a parking garage, etc. etc.

Now Dela's shiny red car, which was only two years old, had a dent on the front passenger side, and scraped paint. But what of Henrik? She'd given him her number, and extracted from him a promise that he would call her to let her know how he was doing, but that night, though the phone rang and rang, it was always someone else. It was funny, they almost never got any calls, and suddenly that night there was a call from Mike Villacrucis way down in Los Angeles, whom they hadn't heard from in almost eight months, telling them how his father had a stroke after breaking the bank at Marapara; and then there was a call from her *Tita* Marilen, up in Daly City, telling them how out of the blue she'd gotten a call from *Manang* Pinky, who apparently had left her husband in the Philippines and come to America on her own, and now needed a place to stay; and then a call from Dale, a friend of her husband's, talking about how his wife, who was six months pregnant with twins, had suddenly contracted chicken pox. But no Henrik. Henrik had disappeared. Maybe he'd lost the scrap of paper on which she'd written her number. Maybe he'd taken it out of his jeans pocket later and found he couldn't read it–God knows her hand had been shaky enough as she'd begun writing her name. She'd written her name on a slip of lined paper torn off a page from a notebook–and even that was strange, because usually she carried a card with her, but that morning she couldn't find it, not anywhere in her handbag. It seemed to have disappeared into thin air. She'd written her name, Dela Lardizabal, and writing it had felt her guilt weigh so palpably on her shoulders that she felt faint, almost as if she could sink to the ground and ask *him*, Henrik, to deliver her to the nearest clinic. Then her number. And, oh God, should she give him her office number, in case this guy turned out to be a crank, one of those loony ones with friends who'd tell him to "sue the bitch for all she's worth!" She was glad her car was dirty–maybe Henrik would think she was just a student. She was glad she had found no card to give him, only a slip of torn paper. But she was sorry, too, about his forearms, and about the nasty shock she had given him. Would she ever be able to set foot in Berkeley again?

She began to have crazy conversations with Henrik in her head. Why didn't you stop, she berated him, over and over. What if something really bad had happened and you got a concussion? Then your wife–or girlfriend, whatever the case may be–would be crying her eyes out right now!

So. For months, she realized, she had expected it to happen. Like the shedding of old clothes. The breaking apart of some outer skin. She'd be standing there on the sidewalk, her two feet in their scuffed, sensible black loafers planted firmly on the ground. She'd be standing there, like some acolyte waiting to be admitted to the feast. Why was she not more prepared? Why was her hair in a mess, flying about her shoulders? Why did she allow her belly, her breasts to sag? Why did her shoulders stoop, why did her eyes dart uneasily from side to side instead of staring straight ahead boldly, confidently?

Other people walked the ground without even paying attention to what they stepped on. It continued to hold them up. No problem. She walked gingerly, as though the earth had a skin one must be careful not to break through. As though there might be something underneath. And everything was fragile. The cup she held in her hand in the kitchen that morning found itself inexplicably on the white tiled floor, shattered into dozens of pieces. Her son, whom she loved and held close at every opportunity, told her stories of things that happened to him at school, stories that tugged at her heart and made her alternately angry, bitter, and sad. Her husband's body, too, seemed to be

161

melting, losing form and definition, assuming a different shape entirely from the one she had grown used to. One evening she watched him working at his computer. He was thin, but his stomach hung loosely over his belt. Why was that? And his face had numerous tiny wrinkles at the corners of his eyes. Noticing this, Dela would run to the mirror in the bathroom and minutely examine her own face, wondering, wondering.

She made an appointment with the Help Center at work. If she thought the ground was in danger of cracking, she might as well talk to someone about it.

She didn't tell her husband. Once, during a fight, she had called his mother in the Philippines, hoping to make him stop shouting. Ever since then, he had called her *sira-ulo*—broken head. She didn't want to give him any more opportunities. She might one day do the inconceivable and run away with their son. She imagined her husband might hire a lawyer. He would then mention that his wife, the broken-head, had once made an appointment to see a "counselor," which she believed was what those people in the Help Center were called.

She didn't know why it didn't make much difference to her that her husband called her such things. When she was growing up, her father often referred to her mother as Idiot Number 1. Her sister was Idiot Number 2, and she was Idiot Number 3. Back home, everyone thought this was wildly funny. Now, she imagined confiding in one of her American friends about this childhood experience. She could imagine the reaction: Pig! Perhaps the word "chauvinist" might precede it. But there you had it.

She made the appointment soon after the accident with the bicyclist. The appointment was with a Dr. Mary Chang. Dec. 3, 1:00. December! She hadn't known it would be that far away, and by then she'd be thinking of Christmas and who knows whether or not she might actually have been swallowed up by the earth by then. They'd find a few strings of her long black hair in the shower stall, and that would be it.

But she found she couldn't wait that long, and one day she

cracked open the yellow pages of the phone book and called various toll-free numbers. At each one, the counselor would begin: Hi! (in that sincere, falsely bright American way) My name is—! What's your name? And Dela would hang up.

Finally, there was one number. A place called the Bridge. A young man answered and didn't ask for her name. He sounded so young. She became suspicious and asked him, "Are you a student?" He admitted he was, and she almost laughed out loud. She, a 33-year-old woman, confiding in this *child*!

Mostly he listened to what Dela had to say, interrupting her narrative only with a non-committal "Ummm, ummm," and there were long stretches when he said nothing at all. After a while, she began to feel strange, as though the voice on the other end of the line was detaching itself slowly from the telephone. Thank you very much, she said abruptly, and hung up. She wondered if he'd been about to say "Ummm."

So she did nothing. And very soon Christmas was almost upon them, and the news that her brother-in-law, a small secretive man who had been living in New York the last five years, would be arriving in San Francisco on the Saturday, and wondered whether he might stay with them? Her husband grumbled–lazy good-for-nothing, he called his brother. All they knew about him was: he worked as a marketing analyst for some unnamed company, and he'd told them that he owned a vacation home in the Catskills, though none of their relatives on the East Coast had ever been invited there and doubted that it actually existed. He rented a room from a Filipino family in Staten Island, and sometimes when Dela called she heard the sound of clanging pots and pans and the hiss of something frying on a stove. She heard an old lady's voice shout her brother-in-law's name, and he would come to the phone out of breath, saying he'd been out back, barbecuing.

But. Still.

She remembered the dark figure in the overcoat who came to the hospital when she was in New York during her brother's dying. He'd come up the elevator to the intensive care ward, where she was sitting in her rumpled clothes on a plastic-covered sofa, and invited her down to the hospital cafeteria, where he bought her a hot dog and cocoa. Sitting across from him at a vinyl-top table, she'd found herself staring with new interest at his face, which did not remind her at all of her husband's. The face that was now in front of her, partially obscured by lazy smoke from his cigarette, was soft all over and in some places pock-marked, and the hair was light brown and thinning at the temples. Only moments earlier, in the intensive care ward, it had seemed to Dela that exhaustion would suck her down, down, right through the linoleum-tiled floor of the waiting lounge. But now she was here, in the cafeteria, her brother-in-law a solid presence, a dark figure in a heavy overcoat who sat silently nodding his head. He did not disappear–in fact, refused to be distressed by Dela's tears. After a while, she began feeling better. As though the hot dog which had sunk like a stone to the pit of her stomach were the only cure she had ever needed. She'd stood up then, made a joke, and later observed how the snowflakes fell on the shoulders of his dark coat as he turned away, towards Lexington Avenue.

Later, back in California, she forgot about him. Doubtless her husband called to let him know the news, but Dela did not care. She lay all day on the bed, a pillow hugged to her stomach. Those days her mouth was stopped up with something vile and bitter that made it impossible for her to talk or even to cry. One day she thought she, too, might be dying, and dragged herself to her car. It was four in the morning. Her husband and son were fast asleep. She drove herself the four miles to the nearest hospital, and by the time she reached the emergency room she was shaking uncontrollably.

"Tell me–is it pneumonia?" she whispered to the young doctor on duty. He'd laughed, then. "No, just the flu," he said. He gave her two Tylenol tablets and sent her home.

She fell asleep on the living room couch. When she awoke the next morning, there was brittle sunlight on her face.

But she is alive! She does not know exactly how or when

the mood of sadness slips from her. She only knows that now she refuses to be sucked under the ground and no longer fears to crack the surfaces of whatever it is she is walking on.

The earth begins to assume solidity. Because of the winter rains the ground is muddy and the mud cakes her boots. She presses gingerly with her toes on the damp ground. She happily tramps around in this mud, as though remembering what it was like to be six or seven years old, walking the streets on rainy afternoons in Manila. She grabs her son's hand firmly as they walk to the park. Sometimes, very occasionally, she will find herself singing. Old songs, from long ago.

"*Leron, leron sinta*—" she will sing. Or, at other times, "*Bahay kubo, kahit munti*—" She does not know where she finds the words. Silly words, really. When her son asks what they mean, she can say only that they are songs she can remember clapping her hands to, in a vine-covered house in Manila.

The next week, she is rear-ended while crossing an intersection along El Camino Real. The hit is hard–so hard she hits the car in front of her, which in turn hits the car in front of it. But when she gets out of the car to take a look, knees shaking, she sees only that the rear bumper is a little askew. Barely scratched, even. While the lady behind her, in the shiny maroon sedan, has a dented hood and a smashed left light. "It's a brand new car, too," the lady says mournfully. And Dela wants to put her arm around the stranger and hug her. But she does not. Instead, when the young policeman asks Dela if she wants to make a report, she shakes her head. Her heart is still beating painfully in her chest, but she forces herself back into her car, and pulls away from the curb without looking back.

SILENCE

Tina's husband liked to bang doors. So when it was silent, very silent in the house, she found herself holding her breath. Don't move, she would whisper to herself. The silence was delicious, pleasurable. It usually lasted for only a minute or two.

Her husband was always checking on her. He didn't like it when she closed their bedroom door, he didn't like not seeing her because then he would think, She is writing in her journal. It was true that she snatched at a little notebook that she kept tucked away under the bed. One day he caught her writing in it, even though she had tried her best to be discreet.

Once he read it without her knowing. She came home from work and he was waiting for her, red-faced. The sound that came out of his mouth was like a bellow. His eyes bulged. He was ugly, then. She thought: How ugly you are. All she could do was bow her head and wait for those seconds of silence when his words were exhausted and she became the merest shadow at the corner of his vision.

At work, papers flew under her nimble fingers. The silence there was not around her but inside. Just under her heart, where no one could see it. Her heart beat painfully loud at times, but she was glad that the sound was dampened by layers of clothes.

People were constantly talking over her head (she was short), through her, around her.

The web site needed a coordinator, she heard someone say. She was very good at html. She heard her supervisor say, "Fine. Use Tina at any time." She found herself grinding her teeth. No one heard the sound of her teeth grinding. If someone were to glance at her just at that moment, they might think she was a little pale, that was all.

———————

One day she was at a little Vietnamese noodle place where all the people from her office liked to go for lunch. She stood in front of the Vietnamese proprietress, who was doing something behind the counter she couldn't quite see–frying egg rolls, perhaps? A hissing sound came from the stove. Though she stood there for what seemed like a very long time, the old woman never looked up. Finally, because she felt embarrassed at standing there so long, she asked the old lady, "Do you have a menu I can look at?" Perhaps she said it with an edge to her voice. She couldn't be sure.

The old lady seemed angry and threw her a brief, scornful glance. "There," she said, gesturing beside the cash box.

Tina reached for the blue sheets, her fingers trembling.

———————

Later the same day, she went to the dry cleaner's. Here the Korean lady was very busy examining the rows of clothes sheathed in plastic. She stood for a while, and finally she pressed a little bell ringer on the counter. The Korean lady gave a frightened start.

"Oh!" she said. "I didn't see you come in! You are so quiet!"

———————

Once she was in New York City. It was the year she'd been laid off from her job of ten years and decided to visit an old schoolmate. Because she was tired and needed to clear her head, she went for a walk. It was early evening. People were coming home from work, their faces blank, their arms full of packages. A block away from her schoolmate's apartment, she saw a "Sale" sign in a clothing store, and went in. She looked only at the "Sale" racks. Finally, she murmured something to the proprietress and this led the proprietress, an Indian woman, to ask her, "Oh, are you a Filipina?" She nodded, yes. "I didn't think so at first," said the Indian lady. "You are too quiet to be a Filipina."

After that she bought a dress. A flowered dress with a skirt that swung around her knees when she moved. She did not want the proprietress to think ill of her.

———————

Before Tina got married, her mother took her out to lunch with a friend she knew only as Tita Fely. Tita Fely had a loud voice. She had hair cut short like a man's. She was married to a handsome tennis instructor and had a beautiful house in Monterey and was raising four sons. Tita Fely looked at her and said, "Don't let your husband push you around. Don't be too good."

———————

When she met her husband, they were both in graduate school. She was very lonely. She didn't know how to cook anything because, back home in Manila, her family had an excellent cook who prepared breakfast, lunch, and dinner. In graduate school, in the high-rise room she shared with a very pale girl who had graduated from Bryn Mawr, she tried to make scrambled eggs by beating a cracked egg in a bowl until her hands got tired. But the frothy mess refused to congeal into the scrambled eggs she knew from back home. She was afraid to boil water, thinking she might set off an explosion. She tried heating dried ramen noodles with hot tap water and they came out tepid and tasteless.

At night she listened to the sounds of her roommate and her roommate's boyfriend, making love in the next room. It confused her that the boyfriend was Chinese but had a name like George. Also that he would prefer this pale white woman to someone Chinese. Her roommate groaned with abandon and she was embarrassed, as if she were doing something bad by listening.

After Tina was married, her mother came from the Philippines at least once a year to visit her. During one of her mother's yearly visits, her mother asked her to drive to Carmel. Tina agreed. That morning, the morning they were to leave, Tina cooked her husband bacon and eggs and rice, his favorite meal. Then she said, "Come and eat." Her husband acted as though he hadn't heard. She had to say it a couple more times before he finally stood up and came to the table.

She didn't think anything of it, but when she looked at her mother, her mother's face was very red. Then Tina was filled with a kind of nameless dread and wanted to get out of the house as quickly as possible.

As they were just about to leave, her husband suddenly said, "Did you tie up the dog?" He had done this before: waited until she was rushing off somewhere, then asked if she had tied up the dog. She always said no, quickly, hurriedly, and he always shook his head as if she had been stupid or careless.

This time she wanted to placate him.

"I'll do it now," she said.

Her mother put a hand on her arm. "Why not let him do it?" Her mother said. "He is not going anywhere."

170

"No, " Tina said, feeling frightened and confused.

"No!" her mother said.

This caused Tina such fear that she bolted out of the house and into the backyard and tied up the dog with three very strong knots.

In the car on the way to Carmel, Tina spent her time looking out the car windows at the cows grazing in the green fields. Her mother suddenly began to tell her a story. It was not a nice story.

In the town of Iloilo, her mother said, when she was growing up, there was a mayor. And this mayor used to beat up his wife.

Tina looked out the window. She thought the countryside reminded her very much of pictures she had seen of England.

Her mother said, "He got so bad he would tie her up."

"And finally," her mother said, "finally he killed her."

It was really a very simple story, but the way her mother paused as she told it seemed to lend it unusual weight and significance.

*reflects Villanueva's writing style

Tina felt something cold and black against her heart.

Why are you telling me this story, she asked her mother.

Are you trying to tell me I will be killed? Are you trying to say I will be tied and beaten up?

Her mother said nothing.

When they arrived in Carmel, Tina was restless. It was a beautiful day. She told her mother, I will go shopping! Her mother had been very quiet in the car after telling her story, and it was important not to let her continue in that mood she had

171

been in. They entered a shop filled with incense and books about Buddhism.

How soothing it is here, Tina thought. She picked up candles and thought of burning them in her bedroom. Her mother said, "What's come over you? Since when have you liked going shopping?"

———————

I tell you this story because nothing happened to Tina. She continued to go to work and to hide her journal from her husband.

One day–she couldn't quite explain it–she wrote in her journal the word "separation", then accidentally left it open on the kitchen counter. When her husband came home that evening, he read it. A silence settled over his features. She was cooking at the stove and had her back turned to him. She listened carefully for the sounds of his footsteps retreating down the hallway.

When he came back to the kitchen, his tie was in his hand. He was standing there in the middle of the kitchen floor without speaking. She made herself turn around and look at him. She actually faced him with her whole body, her back to the stove. They stood facing each other like that for a long moment, neither of them speaking.

MOUNTAINS

Benguet Province, 1950–

The Americans had come and gone; a half-century of colonial rule vanished, in what seemed like the blink of an eye. The bitterness of the Japanese occupation was like a bad taste in the mouth; no one spoke of it, but it was always there, a thickening of the tongue and the membranes.

During this period, a man with a camera roamed the mountains of the high Cordilleras range in northern Luzon. Luzon is a large skull-shaped island in the Philippine archipelago. The skull appears on maps as a profile; the open mouth is formed by Manila Bay. The skull faces east. Invaders from the West came here by rounding the Sea of Celebes. Here and there are dotted numerous islands, too many to be adequately explored. Some are only a mile wide. Deeply forested, these islands were whispered to be the home of giants. No one knows if the stories are true, since, as far as anyone knows, no one has cared to find out. But the Philippine archipelago is full of secrets, secrets it would take a lifetime to uncover.

The man in this story, whose name was Villalon, was in love with the stars and the villages and the muddy mountain pathways. He knew that what he saw through the lens of his camera was truth. To isolate a subject was to transform it. The young woman whom he encountered one day on the hill behind his hut was no longer part of the mountain landscape, no longer part of the green and the sky. She was isolated in his camera lens, frozen, elemental, iconic.

She was Igorot, the strong bones of the mountain people evident in her cheeks, her jaw, her broad shoulders. Her image would live forever.

In the village of Lubuagan, a young girl smiled at him. There were beads in her hair, six clay pots skillfully balanced on the top of her head. Her breasts were firm and round,

173

her calves slightly bowed. Between her feet was a shallow bowl with purple yams. Villalon persuaded her to let him take her picture. He explained that the little box would not capture her spirit and imprison it forever, that it would still be possible for her to speak. In the picture, a naked boy looks at the camera from the shade underneath a nearby hut. Another boy plays in the dirt behind the girl. Blurred chicken shapes dot the smooth-swept courtyard.

The girl smiles directly at the camera, at Villalon. How did he explain about photography, how the images are created? Tricks of light and emulsion, transferred to paper with chemicals. Like sorcery, surely. Villalon was lucky.

Every day he went forth. To Maligcong, Nabanig, Agawa. To Mount Camingingel, Mount Bangbanglang, the Sabangan and Chico Rivers. Spoken out loud, these names sound like an incantation.

His father, Jaime, was a Spanish soldier. His mother was Kankana-ey. She was one of the mountain people. When she married, she was baptized Natividad Pins.

Villalon grew up listening to her stories of the deer leaping on the far-off peaks; of the lizards who turn into men; of the ground-shaking earthquakes. At the time he was born, the first road from the lowlands had just opened up to Baguio City. It was 1929. Driving it was a harrowing and never-to-be-forgotten experience. The narrow, winding, rock-strewn trail hugged rugged cliffs hovering over vicious ravines. Those who attempted it recounted terrifying tales. "Death stalks in front and lurks behind in every foot of the ascent" to the 3,000-foot summit, wrote one intrepid automobilist.

And, not long after the road began to be used, tragedy struck. A large black car moving slowly around a curve in the road plunged suddenly into a ravine, bringing the American senior engineer and his wife with it.

After this inauspicious beginning, the city planners feared that it would be difficult to get people to come to this isolated and mysterious region, enshrouded in cooling mist. Yet, over the years, people did come. A few intrepid souls at first, but later engineers; teachers; businessmen. It would be a place known for its flowers, its fragrant gardens, for Camp John Hay, where there were bowling alleys and steaks, just like in America, where the white-skinned foreigners could find respite from the mosquitoes and the enervating heat of the lowlands. The mountains shuddered from the noise of the heavy machinery.

———————

Then, 1950. Villalon is a young man. It has taken him seven years to graduate from high school. The war and all that, throwing everything into disarray. He worked in a steam laundry in Baguio City. But he had already started taking pictures, as a hobby.

What was happening in Manila in 1950? The Americans had packed up and left, leaving the skeleton of a capital city in the lowlands. Manila, erstwhile Pearl of the Orient, first pulverized by the Japanese and later by MacArthur, in his efforts to re-take it and fulfill his historic promise. *I shall return*, he had said, on the beach at Corregidor.

I would be born eight years later; my parents had not yet met. My mother, only 15, was in a convent school somewhere. My father was 22; he was a young lawyer in Manila, a recent graduate of one of its oldest colleges, the Ateneo University. He drove a red Chevy convertible, a gift from his indulgent father. He listened to Frank Sinatra. He took dancing lessons until the instructor told him he had "heavy feet." Six years later, my father and mother met. Not in Manila, but in New York City, where my mother's family had immigrated, after the war. My father was a young law student in Georgetown.

(I've seen pictures of him from that time. His hair is slicked back. He wears short-sleeved shirts, the sleeves rolled up to show his rather beefy biceps. He wears two-toned shoes.)

What was Manila like in 1950? I've tried to envision it: five years after the war ended, the streets are still filled with heaps of rubble. People are trying to make a living any way they can. Perhaps they've already discovered how to turn the American army jeeps into the modes of public transport we call jeepneys. And companies are starting up: tobacco companies, owned by people like Lucio Tan; glass factories, owned by a former Manila Symphony cellist named Ramon Santa Maria.

Villalon leaves his mountain fastness for a rare trip down to the city. In a secondhand shop he finds a Rolleiflex 2.5 x 2.5 double-lens reflex camera, a great improvement over the heavy single-lens Graflex he has been using. The Graflex has a lens that can be raised and lowered, but it is heavy and inconvenient, requiring glass plates or cut film mounted on holders. The Rolleiflex is lighter, smaller, easier to handle. He can use it to take candid pictures.

The years pass. I don't know what happens from one year to the next, but when I next pick up the thread of Villalon's story, he is married. Like his father he marries a native woman. He has two children. What are these years like for Villalon? They are blurred by an impression of almost continuous, gentle rain. The mountains are very green; so are the rice saplings, springing up from the irrigated terraces the Igorots tended. The green dazzles.

Villalon and his wife open up a photography studio in Baguio City. It is a small, cramped space, but it is all they can afford, with their meager savings. They take pictures of schoolchildren at their First Communion.

The children wear starched white shirts and dresses. They hold candles between palms folded in prayer. Villalon takes pictures of married couples, posing in their Western finery: the men in dark suits, the women in flowered dresses. He always asks them to smile.

When he has time, on weekends, Villalon continues his trips into the interior fastness of valleys and rivers. He does not bring his wife with him.

My first sight of him is in a photograph, circa 1988. Villalon is old. He sits in a rattan chair, gazing solemnly at the camera behind square glasses. His left ankle is heavily taped. It amuses me to see that for this formal portrait, he wore rubber slippers.

And I try to see through his eyes. This is what I think Villalon saw:

May, 1955: In the early mornings, the farmers leading their water buffaloes to the plow. The slow-moving animals appear to be swimming in a sea of brown water. Mud flecks their hairy backs. Their horns stand out white, blinding, against the brown sludge of field and water. The farmers huddle under their thatched capes, hats pulled low to protect them from the early morning rains and the chill. Their shapes move slowly back and forth across the sodden fields. They are like the slow, gentle movements of his wife's hands as she works over her sewing, patiently applying her tiny stitches to a fabric.

June, 1956: It is the planting season, and women are in the fields. Their bare breasts sway pendulously over the dark water. They hold the rice saplings tenderly in their fists. A salakot, the round native hat, shades their faces. Villalon finds that, in the presence of such innocence, his palms begin to sweat and he has to grip his camera more firmly.

April, 1957: It is the dry season now, and in a village called Malegkong a young man crouches on a hillside, playing a nose flute. The leaves of a fragrant camias tree are plaited in his hair. A buri cloth bag is slung over his back. His eyes gaze out, expressionless, at the rice terraces.

September, 1958: They are harvesting rice again in Buscalan. Here the old women move, bare-breasted, through the fields. Their backs are wide and flat. Slung around their hips are small baskets for catching edible insects. The women laugh to see him approach with the strange box in his hands. But they already know about him, so they don't stop what they are doing.

At the end of the day, the harvested rice is carried to the villages on two baskets slung on a pole. The men move stiffly, the pole punishing their bare shoulders.

At the end of the day, the villagers sit outside their huts, smoking pipes. What do they talk about with Villalon? Do they talk about stars and of enchantments? About women who venture into the forests alone and turn into deer? Or is the talk only of mundane things like rain: whether it will come or not come. About rice. About the city on the other side of the mountain.

While men sharpen knives or spearheads, the women sit close by, crooning to babies held tightly in their arms. Children play in the dirt. Pigs roam the spaces underneath the houses. The mountain dogs with their sharp teeth gnaw uselessly at pieces of bone.

The villagers ask themselves, Who is this man? The man with the box that takes magic pictures? The box that captures likenesses, freezes them in an eternal captivity? They are not sure what he is. He is so tall and white, and his clothes are of the lowlands. And yet, when he opens his mouth to speak, the words that come pouring out are in their language.

In time, they grow to forget about him. They pick each other's lice not two feet away from his lens. The women let him into their houses. He sits at their hearths and gnaws hungrily on their offerings of roasted pigs' hooves. A family lets him watch as they prepare their meal in a large clay pot resting on three stones. He notices the look of pensive reverie on all their faces, even the youngest, as they stare into the fire. Hunger—the same hunger that causes their bellies to shrivel up tight and hard—makes them quiet. No one looks at the photographer, busy with his box in a corner.

The old women weave tirelessly, cloths with lizard and crocodile emblems. He watches their old gray heads, the snakebone headdresses, symbols of fertility, wound around their gray hair. A grandchild or two curls up peacefully at their feet. The old women croon an old ballad:

The warrior has been away
For a long time;
He has left since many planting seasons.
He has not returned.
He has not gone home.
Because of this, we long for brotherhood;
For this reason,
We seek friendship.

He jots down the words in a journal. There is a hunger in him—he can't explain it—a hunger to reclaim their language, their words, their dreams. Perhaps it is because he remembers his mother, the native girl Cunyap who was re-named Natividad Pins. Perhaps he noticed a sadness in her dark eyes.

One day Villalon watches a well-built man dressed only in a loincloth, engaged in weaving a hat. The work takes the man almost the entire day: cutting the rattan into fine long strips takes a very long time. The man looks down in utter concentration. Not once does he look up at the photographer. Not once does he open his mouth to speak.

Villalon, too, does not move, though his belly growls with hunger. He is intent, with a kind of devotion that seems like prayer.

Why were all these secrets revealed to Villalon? One day, he did not go back to his wife. He remained there, in one of the villages, in a small hut. He was sick, feverish. He'd been attacked by a pack of fierce dogs. They had torn open his arm. It took many weeks for the wounds to heal. At the end of that time, Villalon was a different person. He no longer wanted to go back to Baguio and operate a photography studio.

His wife sent her brothers to plead with him. But they came back, shaking their heads. They told her, it would be best

179

to forget about him. He is not the man you knew. Villalon's wife, bowing her head, submitted to her fate.

———————

Villalon grew old. He was so old that he didn't know what to do with his arms and legs. But he would not leave this country of the rugged mountains and the rice fields. The green had burned into his brain, as an image imprints on film. He knew he would die here.

Before he realized it, his hands curved around his old camera came to resemble claws. He had not lost any of his avidity and went out among the Igorots. Once or twice a young girl came home with him. Lying next to their supple bodies in his hut, he imagined a life for himself, in another body: the body he imagined for himself was young and strong and brown, with corded muscles in the legs that allowed him to leap from boulder to boulder along the mountainsides. He had a throat that could sing in the frigid mountain air. He had children, little Igorot babies, crowding around his feet. In the mornings, he always awoke alone, the space next to him on the mat already cold.

Yet he could not leave.

The wife in the city of Baguio—even her sadness could not touch him. He was lost.

One day, a doctor from the lowlands came to see him.

"Villalon", the doctor said. "You are so old. Don't you want to live down there with your people?"

Villalon looked at him. The doctor heard only the silence resounding in the little hut. After a while, he took his hat and his cane and left with stooped shoulders. The Igorots watched him leave.

Don't you know, they wanted to tell the doctor. Don't you know that Villalon has been enchanted. He could never leave, even if he wanted to. Our women have spit in his food and our children scattered dirt among his clothes, the clothes he washed in the stream. We old folk drew his spirit out like a skein. The women wove it into the lizard patterns in their skirts. He is trapped there forever, under the lizard's tail.

The old people could already see his bones, white, in the burial urn. They knew which cave they would put him in. Not the cave of their ancestors, where the bones rested in lovingly decorated jars, facing a great promontory that looked out over a valley. They knew they would put Villalon in a hollow in the mountain that no one would ever see. And the pictures from the magic box would be burned in an offering to his spirit.

©2002 Stella Kalaw

Marianne Villanueva has been writing and publishing stories about the Philippines and Filipino Americans since the mid-1980s. Her critically acclaimed first collection of short fiction, *Ginseng and Other Tales from Manila* (Calyx Books 1991) was short-listed for the Philippines' National Book Award. Her work has been widely anthologized. Her story, "Silence," first published in The Threepenny Review, was short-listed for the 2000 O. Henry Literature Prize. Most recently, she has edited an anthology of Filipina women's writings, *Going Home to a Landscape,* which was selected as a Notable Book by the prestigious Kiriyama Pacific Rim Book Prize. She currently teaches writing and literature at Foothill College and Notre Dame de Namur University. Born and raised in Manila, she now lives in the San Francisco Bay Area.